Mysterious Monday

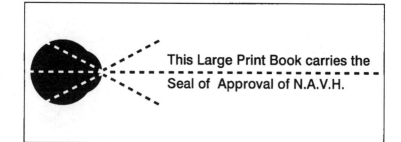

Mysterious Monday

Juli Scott Super Sleuth
Book 1

Colleen L. Reece

Thorndike Press • Thorndike, Maine

Published in 2001 by arrangement with Colleen L. Reece.

Thorndike Press Large Print Christian Mystery Series.

The tree indicium is a trademark of Thorndike Press.

The text of this Large Print edition is unabridged.
Other aspects of the book may vary from the original edition.

Set in 16 pt. Plantin by Minnie B. Raven.

Printed in the United States on permanent paper.

ISBN 0-7862-3068-1 (lg. print : hc : alk. paper)

Mysterious Monday

Chapter 1

Juli Scott hit the snooze button on her digital clock and burrowed deep beneath the pale yellow comforter that matched her bedroom walls. Nine wonderful minutes stretched ahead, her favorite time of day and often the only nine minutes in which she could daydream. "Aspiring authors, especially aspiring mystery authors, need to daydream," she mumbled. Dark-blue eyes squeezed shut, she easily entered the wonderful world of fantasy.

"Tell me, Miss Scott," the cynical host of "Northwest Happenings" asked. "How does it feel to be Bellingham, Washington's pretty, blond answer to Carolyn Keene?" He smiled toothily at the camera. "For any listener out there who isn't groovy, Carolyn Keene was the little old lady who wrote the Nancy Drew series of teen mysteries."

Groovy! Juli choked back a giggle. If Ed Cunningham wanted to be credible, he'd better learn slang that didn't go out with the dinosaurs. She clutched sweaty hands and wished she'd never agreed to this interview. Dad had warned her about how rude and patronizing Cunningham was to his guests. She bit her lip. "I don't consider myself —"

"There no need to act coy," Cunningham cut in. He turned his super-white smile her way. "How many teenagers" (he pronounced the word as if it were some kind of disease) "win a writing contest sponsored by a major publisher and have a book published?" He held up a brightly colored volume. "Mysterious Monday. *Cute."*

Instead of intimidating Juli, his sarcasm stiffened her backbone. From early childhood she had always hated heroines who were nothing more than victims in disguise. Anger licked at her veins and crisped her voice. "The contest was for young adult writers and the book isn't 'cute,' Mr. Cunningham. It's a story that could actually happen."

"Really?" He raised a disbelieving eyebrow.

Juli felt she had scored a point but Ed Cunningham changed tactics. His next question caught her off guard. She recognized it as retaliation for her spurt of defiance.

"I understand you're a Christian." Cunningham pointed an accusing finger at the

dust jacket. "How do you justify writing about crime?"

A silent prayer shot up from Juli's heart. She hesitated — and saw the triumph in her adversary's gloating face. Was this why she had been invited to appear on "Northwest Happenings"? So Cunningham could show her up as a hypocrite and make a mockery of Christianity? Not on his life!

She took a deep breath and demanded, "Why not? All of us, including Christians, live surrounded by crime." She pointed at Mysterious Monday and gave Cunningham a deceptively sweet smile. "You must be aware from reading the book that it doesn't glorify crime or make it sound macho or cool in any way."

Bingo! Admitting he hadn't bothered to read the book before interviewing its author meant losing popularity with his viewers. Cunningham hastily changed the subject. Again. "Mmm, quite commendable. Now about the ending. Even you must admit it is unbelievable, even bizarre."

Juli felt her mouth widen in an irrepressible smile. Mischief flowed through her. This was beginning to be fun. "Unbelievable?" She leaned forward and took the offensive. "It's been said if life were a stage play, no one would come, because it's so unbelievable. I *won't give away the ending and spoil* Mysterious Monday *for those who haven't read it, but . . ."*

Juli's nine minutes ended with a wail of the alarm. She stretched. "Just when it was getting good." She wondered while showering why her daydream had taken such a strange twist. Nothing mysterious about this Monday.

Juli toweled off and reached for the blow dryer that made a halo of her shoulder-length, blondish-brown hair. Thank goodness she didn't bother with much makeup. She'd have to give up her precious nine minutes plus a whole lot more. She ran a lipstick over her mouth, climbed into jeans and her favorite blue sweater, then opened the mini-blinds. A pale wintry sun fought encroaching clouds. Looked like there might be a little snow. *Great!* A few inches of the white stuff meant tons of it on Mt. Baker. Maybe Dad would take her and Mom skiing over the weekend.

"Breakfast, Juli." Mom's voice floated down the hall.

"Coming." Juli hurried to the blue-and-white kitchen she liked almost as well as her own sunny bedroom. Anne Scott, an older edition of her daughter, brightened the

10

kitchen with her jeans and scarlet sweatshirt that read, *HFC: Homemaker First Class.* "How come you're so much younger and better-looking than my friends' mothers?" Juli teased, hugging her.

"Ha! You only say that because I look like you." Mom deftly scooped scrambled eggs from the pan onto blue-banded plates, then added crisp toast to each. "Pour the juice, will you, please?" Mom balanced the plates and stepped through the wide arch that led to the adjoining dining room.

"Sure." Juli grabbed a crystal pitcher from the refrigerator and followed. A multitude of blooming house plants in the window drank in every ray of light possible. Rainbows from several sun-catchers danced on pale green walls, reminding Juli of an early spring walk in the forest. She hungrily eyed the inviting plates of food, crystal dish of raspberry jam, and sparkling white tablecloth. "Colorful."

"My darling daughter," an amused voice drawled from the doorway. "How many times must your mother tell you there's nothing like a pretty table setting, good breakfast, and cheerful company —"

"— to help get the day off to a good start," Juli finished.

"I could go back to teaching and leave you

to eat frozen waffles and dry cereal," Mom solemnly announced. A twinkle in her eyes betrayed the humor behind the threat.

"A fate worse than death!" Gary Scott's gray eyes took on a look of horror, even though his mouth twitched. He stepped into the room, tall, dark-haired, and commanding in his Washington State Patrol uniform. "I hear enough griping on the job from people who start out their days in that kind of rush." He dropped a light kiss on Juli's hair, squeezed Mom's shoulders, then took his place at the head of the table. "You'll never know how glad I am we have an old-fashioned family with God at the head and you at the heart, Anne."

Juli felt warmed by his deep voice. Her parents were the best. Would she have a home someday, and a husband who looked at her with the deep love and respect she saw in Dad's eyes? The idea left her breathless.

Mom and Dad held out their hands to her. In the moment before Dad began to pray, Juli said her own private prayer. It might be old-fashioned for Mom to make a career out of caring for her family and being a good neighbor, but it was what she and Dad wanted. *Me too, God,* Juli silently added.

"Thank You for another day in which to

serve You, Lord." Dad's rich voice sounded loud and strong in the quiet room. "We give You praise. Thank You for our food, for our family. Help us to be witnesses and touch the lives of others, not only this day, but always. In Jesus' name, amen."

A sharp, insistent ring shattered the silence. The pleasant breakfast ended almost before it started. "Already?" Mom looked distressed, but Dad just raised his eyebrows and stepped into the kitchen. Juli heard him say, "Just a minute. I'll put you on hold and take it in the den."

Juli sighed. "That means no breakfast for him." How many meals and family times had been interrupted by the annoying scream of the phone or doorbell?

"It's my job, honey," Dad reminded on his way to the hall.

"I know." Only too well. Juli didn't voice her suspicions, but she had the feeling Dad had recently become involved in some kind of hush-hush stuff. As a policeman's daughter, she knew better than to ask. Some things he couldn't share even with his family. No longer hungry, she made a pretense of eating for Mom's sake and waited, one ear cocked to the low conversation in the den.

Dad came back wearing a heavy jacket,

hat in hand. "I may be late." He bent, swiftly kissed Mom, then tousled Juli's hair. "See you." A few long strides and the kitchen door closed behind him.

"See you." Juli heard the garage door go up, the sound of the patrol car starting. "Mom, do you ever wish Dad did something else?"

"Of course." She rose and began clearing away dishes. "On the other hand, I knew when I married him how much he felt God needed caring persons in his profession. No one will ever know how much good he does. I'm proud of your father. He faces danger every day so the world will be a safer place for the rest of us."

"I'm proud, too," Juli whispered. "It's just that sometimes I get scared. Dumb, huh, when Dad's always been a policeman."

Her mother sat back down, eyes bluer than a mountain lake. "Fear is never dumb, Juli, but it is crippling. All we can do is leave him in God's hands." She smiled tremulously. "I can't think of a better place, can you?"

"No." Juli felt better. "Thanks for the pep talk." She knew Mom had spoken as much to her own fears as to Juli's.

Snow began falling a little after noon. By the time school dismissed and Juli stepped down from her bus, the storm had intensified to near-blizzard proportions. How dark it was for this time of day, even in January! Had something happened to the street lights? "Uh-oh. Electricity's out." She struggled the short distance home from her stop, thankful she'd been smart enough to wear her fleece-lined jacket and heavy, laced boots.

In contrast to the dimly lit homes around it, the Scotts's yellow ranch-style house with its white shutters and window boxes looked like a scene from a Christmas card. Snow hung on every fir and hemlock. It formed jaunty caps on the gateposts and roof. A steady, welcoming light shone through the spotless living room windows between partly open drapes.

Leave it to Mom! No puny candlelight for her. As far back as Juli could remember, a row of shining glass lamps had stood on a convenient garage shelf just outside the kitchen door. Mom kept them sparkling clean at all times, filled with oil, and wicks trimmed.

"Just like the story in the Bible," Juli told her every time the electricity went off and they resorted to lamplight. "No storm will catch you unprepared, like one of those five foolish maidens!"

She repeated it when she stood dripping

15

on the tile floor of the small entryway, then called, "Acting out Bible stories again? Mmmm. Do I smell stew?"

"You better believe it!" Mom came from the kitchen, carrying a huge kettle. "I had it nearly cooked before we lost power. It can finish in here." She set the stew on the fireplace insert. It continued to bubble and send forth a welcoming aroma.

Her face looked flushed and pretty. Anticipation lit her eyes. "Family night tonight." She giggled like a child. "I actually like it when there's no power."

"So do I, if Dad's here," Juli said. She quickly amended, "I mean, we have a good time when it's just us, but Dad makes it even better."

Some of Mom's radiance dimmed. "He warned us he might be late, but I hope things turn out differently." She walked to the window.

Juli joined her. Swirling snow hid everything except the small piece of yard directly in front of the living room window. "Pretty, though."

"Yes." Anne Scott shivered. "I think we'll draw the drapes. Gary will come in the driveway and through the kitchen door."

An hour limped by.

Then another.

16

At six-thirty, Mom said they'd better eat. The stew proved every bit as appetizing as it smelled. Juli took seconds. Her skimpy breakfast and cafeteria lunch felt days away. "It seems funny not to be using the dishwasher," Mom said later, hands deep in detergent suds. "Thank goodness for a gas water heater. At least we have hot water for dishes and bathing."

"Right." Juli dried a plate. A storm-muffled noise outside sent her to the kitchen window. She pushed back the blue, country-print curtains and peered out. "Dad's here. I'm glad the stew is still hot."

"So am I." Mom snatched a towel and wiped her hands. "Bring a lamp, Juli. We'll have to release the garage door opener, so the door can be put up manually." They hurried out. Juli set the lamp on a shelf. Mom pulled the release. Together they pushed up the heavy door.

A tall, snow-covered figure stepped inside. Until that moment, Juli hadn't known how much she wanted Dad home and safe from the storm. Heedless of his wet coat, she threw herself against him. "I'm so glad you're here!"

Strong arms convulsively tightened around her, then gently pushed her away. "Sorry."

"Who — ?" Amazed, she fell back.

"Gary?" Mom grabbed the lamp from the shelf and came to them.

"No. It's Brian Baker." A howling gust of wind swept into the open garage and nearly extinguished the lamp, but not before Juli recognized her father's partner, face shadowed by the flickering light.

Mom recovered first. "Close the garage door, Brian, and come in."

An eternity passed before the heavy door shut out some of the raging night. Brian threw aside his coat, leaving it and his boots in the garage. In the well-lit kitchen, Juli had trouble believing he could be her father's partner and close friend. Where was the handsome trooper, a few years younger than Dad, but one of the best on the force? This man looked old and sick, as if he had been dealt a mortal blow.

"Where's Dad?" Juli clutched his arm. "Is he coming soon?"

Patrolman Baker's mouth trembled. He shook his head. "No."

"Did he say when?" Mom forced a laugh and Juli's fingers tightened on the rigid arm. "We can't keep the stew warm forever."

He ignored the feeble joke and licked pallid lips. When he finally spoke, the words were so low Juli had to strain to hear them.

"Mrs. Scott, Juli . . ." His breathing grew harsh, unnatural. "Gary won't be coming soon." Baker's face contorted into a ghastly caricature. "He won't be coming at all."

Chapter 2

"Not coming home!" Juli's hand fell from Brian Baker's arm. *What do you mean?*

The young state patrol officer bowed his head.

Anne Scott's face turned the color of ashes. "Was it an accident?"

"Was *what* an accident?" Juli's voice rose to a shriek.

Baker looked up. "I received special permission to be the one to come tell you Gary is gone. I can say no more." His words sounded mechanical, robotlike.

"We have a right to know what happened," Mom said in a stunned voice. "It's bad enough to have your husband die in the line of duty. Not to know how or why is unbearable!"

Her protest did no good. The patrolman turned and bolted into the garage. The door went up, down, then thudded to the floor with sickening finality.

"Dad is *dead?*" Juli's stomach heaved. She got to the bathroom just in time. Mom followed, putting aside her shock and grief to help her daughter. When it was over, she bathed Juli's face with a damp cloth. "We've always known it might happen. We've been a couple of ostriches, pretending it couldn't."

"That's it? You're just going to accept it? Dad can't be dead. It doesn't make sense. Why would God let someone die who's out helping people? Call headquarters, Mom. Tell them we have to know . . ." Her voice faltered, tears coming in a flood.

After a night of unspeakable horror, in spite of the comforting presence of their hastily called pastor, Anne and Juli braved the icy streets and arrived at state patrol headquarters.

"We have to know," they insisted, right up through the chain of command to the highest-ranking official. His kindly face showed compassion, but he proved as inflexible as a solid steel bar and told them behind locked doors, "We simply cannot give you details, Mrs. Scott. Because your husband was such a fine officer, I will tell you this much, although doing so is risky: Your husband was secretly working on something that could endanger many lives, perhaps even yours and your daughter's."

So I was right, Juli thought. It brought neither triumph nor comfort.

"Gary Scott gave his best, at a terrible cost," the officer continued. "Will you accept my word for that and let the rest of it lie? If not, his sacrifice was meaningless."

"What choice do we have?" Juli sullenly demanded.

Mom gave her a reproving glance and nodded in acceptance. They left headquarters in silence. Juli passively agreed with whatever Mom said, too numb to care until something happened that set her brain whirling.

They received official word the casket would remain closed.

"Why?" Juli asked herself. "Why would they give such an order?" Suspicion exploded inside her. What if the whole thing were a diabolical plot? *Sure,* a little voice inside scoffed, *the state patrol has nothing better to do than attend phony funerals.* Yet no matter how much she told herself otherwise, Juli stubbornly clung to the frail thread of hope. Stranger things have happened. *Look at all the unexplained mysteries on TV. Just maybe this will be one of them.*

Juli's outlandish idea actually helped her make it through the funeral. Even false hope seemed better than admitting Dad wouldn't be coming home ever again. She'd tried to pray, but felt either she or God had moved. If she could figure out which, maybe she'd feel close to Him, the way she had from childhood until Patrolman Baker's visit last week. She didn't dare tell Mom, but secretly wished she could.

Lines that had not been there a week earlier appeared in Anne's face. One evening she said, "We have to make plans. Your dad saw to it we'd be provided for, just in case." Her chin trembled. "We'll keep the house, of course. Our lawyer advises paying off the mortgage." Her gaze traveled around the spacious living room, out the window to the snow-clad lawn that made up the half-acre lot, and back to the wood paneled walls and fireplace insert open to show leaping flames. "I'm also going to take courses and renew my teaching certificate. I don't think I can stand being alone here all day."

She looked so vulnerable in the glow of the firelight, Juli impulsively got up from the couch and hugged her. Juli began to understand that with death comes a lot more than a funeral. She'd never considered they might lose their home. And Mom would be working — no more homemade cinnamon rolls or Mom being there when she got home. Pain washed away some of the numbness that had protected her, drowning even the shame for her selfish thoughts.

Mom must have read her mind. "We'll do special meals on weekends."

"I don't have to be in so many after-school activities." A sinking feeling attacked Juli's middle. "I'll come straight home and —"

Mom shook her head. "We'll have simpler meals. You need a life. Get it?"

"Got it." Juli felt secretly relieved, although the newly discovered aching only worsened. "It doesn't sound easy."

A frown marred Mom's smooth forehead. "It won't be, but God will help."

Then why didn't He help when Dad needed Him so much? Juli bit her tongue to keep from asking. Besides, she didn't know for sure He hadn't. The mystery of not knowing what happened, and of the closed casket, had never been resolved. Suspicion suddenly overwhelmed her.

"I don't believe Dad is dead," she blurted out.

"Why, Juli!" Mom looked at her as if she'd just flown in from Mars.

"If Dad really is dead, I'd know it in here." She put one hand over her heart. The next moment all the tears she should have shed at the funeral came.

Mom grabbed a box of tissues and pulled

Juli into her lap. "It's okay," she whispered. "Even Jesus wept." They cried together for a long time, using up most of the tissues.

Finally Juli straightened and sniffled a last time. "I guess I'm losing it."

"No way." Mom gave her a bleary-eyed smile and mopped at Juli's face. "Everything we're feeling is natural and part of the healing process."

"I thought maybe I was headed for the funny farm."

"Not you. You're a survivor. We both are." Mom's smile curled into Juli's heart like a kitten toasting his paws before a blazing fire. "By the way, I have a present for you, if you'll let me up."

Juli obligingly slid to the floor and sat cross-legged on the rug. Mom went to the spare bedroom she'd been using, returned, and tossed Juli a square box.

"Must not be breakable." Juli untied the perky red plaid ribbon, reached inside and touched something soft and furry.

"He's adorable!" Juli cuddled the brown plush teddy bear whose shiny black eyes stared at her as if pleading to be loved. She held him away from her, tied the plaid ribbon around his neck, then hugged him again. "Thanks, Mom. I love him. Does he have a name?"

Mischief sparkled in Mom's eyes and she looked more like her old self. "I thought a budding author might like to have a companion named Clue to sit on her desk and inspire her."

"Clue is perfect." Emotionally exhausted but more at peace than she'd been since the blizzard, Juli repeated, "Thanks, Mom," and hugged her new friend.

Weeks later, she glanced up from her homework and noticed her mother's changing expressions. Now Anne Scott studied as hard as her daughter. She had carried out her plans and was earning high grades in her college classes. Juli stroked Clue's soft fur until Mom looked up and smiled, then she asked, "How did you know I needed someone to hug when you weren't around?"

"I'm your mother."

"Go to the head of the class," Juli told her.

Mom chuckled. "I won't if I don't finish my homework. I won't get a teaching job, either. Sorry to have to leave you, but I need to go use the computer." She ruffled her daughter's hair and headed for the den.

"Leave the door open," Juli called, as usual. The sound of the computer made the house feel friendlier.

"Just so it doesn't disturb your studying or beauty sleep," Mom called back.

"Implying I need all I can get!"

"Did I say that?" A cocked eyebrow betrayed Mom's amusement before she disappeared down the hall.

Juli slowly followed with Clue, but stopped at her own room and sat on the edge of the bed. Somewhere in the distance, a siren screamed. She shivered and wrapped her arms tightly around her faithful bear. When Dad had been home, sirens never bothered her. But after the funeral, though too ashamed to tell anyone, she stiffened every time she heard their mournful cry. It took weeks of fighting her fears to find a way to confront and deal with them.

Now she closed her eyes and whispered, "Please, God, be with anyone who is in trouble," as she did each time a siren wailed. She slowly relaxed. A smile trembled on her sensitive lips. What would the Bellingham firefighters, police, and ambulance crews think if they knew a fifteen-year-old girl said a prayer each time she heard the wail of a siren?

"They'll never know," she reassured herself. "Neither will whoever might be hurt or in trouble. I will, though. You too, God." Gradually, her heartbeat slowed to normal, and a gentle peace settled over her.

Juli lay back and stared at the ceiling. Why

was it easier to pray for people she didn't know and probably never would, than for herself? She knew God loved her and things had gradually become a little better between them. Yet too many unanswered questions had shaken her former confidence that He heard and answered even the smallest prayer. She longed for the carefree days before Dad was gone, then sighed, and rolled off the bed. It was getting late and she had a chemistry test coming up in the morning.

Day by day, week by week, winter gave way to spring. Juli and her mother silently packed away their ski equipment. Mom had suggested going once, but the weather warmed that weekend, bringing the danger of avalanches. Juli felt relieved. Not enough time had passed for her to hit the slopes. She knew if she went now, she'd see her father's flying figure on every run; hear his booming laugh when he took a spill and coasted downhill on his face.

"The firsts are the worst," she told Dr. Marlowe when she went in for a routine checkup before spring sports began. Always comfortable with the doctor she'd known since her toddler days, Juli felt she could talk frankly with the older woman, especially about feelings. "You know what I mean," she continued. "Like the first time

Mom and I went to a favorite restaurant without Dad. Or to church. That kind of stuff. The next time's a whole lot easier."

"It takes a wise person to figure that out," the doctor said. "Of course, some things catch you when you aren't prepared. Has that happened?"

"Twice," Juli admitted. She dug the toe of one Nike into her other arch. "Once when I saw Brian Baker." She frowned. "He hardly ever comes around. Maybe he feels too awful. Or maybe he feels guilty about what-ever happened." She didn't add anything about what the superior officer had told her and Mom of Gary Scott's undercover activi-ties.

"The other time was when one of Dad's favorite songs played on the car radio. I started to turn it off, but Mom said let it play. We both bawled, but then we felt better."

"Good." Dr. Marlowe clasped her smooth hands together. "Tears are part of healing. So are the unexpected moments that bring them." She stood. "I'm proud of you and your mother, Juli. You're a couple of win-ners."

Juli left the office, deep in thought. Should she forget her dream of being a mys-tery writer and go into medicine? Look at all the good Dr. Marlowe did. The next moment she muttered, "I don't think so. I'd probably pass out at my first operation. Besides, I don't even like TV hospital shows!"

Summer came, and with it, a new kind of normal in the Scott household. June gave way to July before they were hit with another bombshell. Juli arrived home from a walk one day to find her mother seated at the kitchen table. Several closely typed pages, including what looked like street maps, lay spread out before her, crowding the fruit bowl to the edge of the table. "What's that, homework?" Juli asked. She grabbed an apple and leaned over Mom's shoulder.

"I wish." Mom looked devastated.

Juli's stomach lurched. She put down the apple. "The state isn't planning to evict us, tear down the house, and build a freeway, are they?"

Mom managed a weak smile. "Not quite that bad, although you may think so." She handed Juli the top page of a letter.

Juli scanned it. "So the school district is chopping up the city into little pieces, only they call it 'redistribution.' This doesn't affect me, does it?"

Mom looked troubled. "Unfortunately, it does."

"You mean I have to transfer?" Juli exploded. "I can't! Nine years plus kindergarten with the same kids and now I get shoved into a new school? No way!" She grabbed the map and studied it with disbelieving eyes. "Mom, I'm practically the only one from Cove who will be going to Hillcrest!"

Mom looked sympathetic. "You make friends easily. Besides, Hillcrest is beautiful and only a year old."

"It's chopped liver," Juli flatly stated. "I'd rather have Cove — it's old and ivy-covered, but it's my school. Who needs transplanting when they're already growing great?" She thought of the assembly room at Cove, lined with pictures of honor students, athletes, star debaters. She had her fair share and more among them. A flicker of pride gave way to hopelessness. "Fat chance I have of getting into any activities at Hillcrest. All the sophomores who were freshmen there last year are ahead of me. Can't we get a special exemption or something?"

"Only if we can prove you're a hardship case."

Juli's hopes soared. "Leaving my friends is definitely a hardship."

Mom turned a page. "It says here no one need apply for an exemption unless it causes financial problems or undue travel time. We can't plead either. We're over the financial minimum and Hillcrest is closer than Cove. Sorry, Juli." She sighed. "I know you're disappointed. I am, too, but there's no alternative."

Juli ran from the kitchen to the shelter of her own room. Clutching Clue, she curled into a ball on her bed. "Where are You when I need You, God?" She knew she was being unreasonable, but didn't care. "You could have stopped this from happening." A sob tore from her throat. "Thanks a whole bunch."

Chapter 3

Early September morning sunlight poured through the raised mini-blinds of Juli's bedroom. It reflected on her pale yellow walls and matching comforter. "So what?" Juli always said when friends urged her to redecorate in more contemporary colors: black; silver; gold; bright pink. "I like yellow. It's a happy color." *And familiar,* she always mentally added.

It didn't help today. Neither did a glimpse of herself in the mirror. Why had she ever bought this flowered skirt and blue T-shirt? She started to take them off, but shook her head. She'd already changed clothes three times and the accusing red numerals on her digital clock showed she was running out of time.

Juli sat on her bed, hugged Clue, and stared at the room. "It's not the room or my clothes," she told her furry friend. "It's me. I haven't felt this way since Mom dropped me off for my first day of kindergarten. I know it's stupid. I'm almost sixteen years old, not five." She closed her eyes. "Please, God . . ."

She couldn't go on. Her anger over being transferred from Cove to Hillcrest had been replaced with the knowledge she couldn't do a thing about it, but she still found it hard to pray.

"Breakfast, Juli," Mom called.

Her reluctant daughter slid off the bed, smoothed it, set Clue in his usual spot, and headed down the hall. She took a deep breath just outside the kitchen doorway and pasted on a smile.

"Where's my hug?" Mom asked.

Juli's eyes opened wide. No sweatshirt and jeans for her mother today. "You look great!"

"Thanks." Anne hugged Juli and slowly turned to model her new white blouse and tailored red slacks. "I thought we'd eat breakfast in here during the week."

Juli took a chair at the already laid table in front of the window. "Good."

Her mind raced while Mom asked the blessing. She'd been so caught up in her own misery, she hadn't stopped to realize what today meant to Mom. Getting back into teaching wouldn't be easy. Mom was bound to struggle with all the changes that had taken place in the education system during her long absence as a Homemaker First Class.

"Earth to Juli. Come in, Juli. Time, tides, congealing eggs, and your bus wait for no one." Anne laughed and shadows from the past fled the cozy kitchen.

Juli sheepishly returned to the present. "Sorry."

Mom drank the last of her juice and glanced at the kitchen clock. "I have to run." She slipped into the bright red blazer that matched her pants. "I'm glad I found a job teaching first-graders. They love bright colors as much as I do."

"I can see you thirty years from now," Juli teased. "Snow-white hair above clothes of emerald, sapphire, and ruby red."

"Down with drab, I always say." Mom dropped a kiss on the top of Juli's head. "Thanks for clearing. See you tonight."

"Bye." As soon as her mother went out, Juli dumped her breakfast. Even Mom's banana muffins wouldn't mix well with the butterflies in her stomach. She cleaned up the kitchen and slowly walked toward her bus stop, feeling low.

"It isn't fair." She kicked at a stone and watched it go flying. The action relieved some of her tension, but when she got off the bus at Hillcrest, things went from bad to worse. She caught a glimpse of John Foster, Ted Hilton, his sister Amy, and Dave Gilmore just outside the front doors. The tiny blond had her head thrown back and was laughing up into Dave's face.

Juli's mood went from dark to midnight black. Why did Amy Hilton have to get transferred to Hillcrest? John and Ted were okay. And Dave . . . she felt warmth creep into her face. Dave never paid her much attention, but Juli secretly had liked him since junior high. She took comfort in the fact he hadn't paid much attention to other girls, either. Probably too busy with school, sports, and church youth activities, or maybe a little shy. It certainly wasn't because girls didn't like him, she knew.

Juli surveyed Dave the way she did characters for her stories. Hair: brown and short. Eyes: bright blue. Smile: warmer than Mom's homemade gingerbread. Height: about 6 feet. (Juli, herself at 5'7", had to look up several inches to meet his gaze the few times she'd stood near him in the cafeteria.) Build: muscular, but lean.

Dave looked away from Amy's upturned face and over the laughing, shoving crowd. Did he sense someone was watching him? Juli panicked, ducked her head, and stepped behind a taller student. The last thing she needed was for Dave Gilmore to catch her spying on him. By the time she found the courage to look again, Amy and the three boys had become part of the mass surging through the doors. Juli waited until the crowd thinned out, then stepped into the corridor that stretched ahead of her for what looked like miles.

"Julianne?" a man's voice called from an open doorway.

Juli cringed. Mom's name tacked onto Juli definitely was not cool. A few snickers from nearby students showed they agreed. She turned, recognizing the short, friendly looking principal she had met briefly when she came to register.

"Come in, please." He motioned her into the office marked *Mr. S. Miles.* Juli knew the *S* stood for Samuel, but the kids called him Mr. Smiles behind his back. It fit. His face shouted his hopes for a school filled with happy campers.

"Sit down, Julianne. I've heard such good reports about you from your previous school, I'd like to ask a favor." He settled behind his desk like a mother hen on her nest.

Flattery will get you everywhere, Juli thought sourly as she slumped into a chair. Oh, well. At least someone at Hillcrest knew who she was.

Mr. Smiles didn't seem to notice her silence or the way she nervously rubbed sweaty palms together. "We have a new student who needs to be shown around. She's going to have a pretty hard time of it at first, coming from so far away."

Juli felt her mouth drop open. He was asking *her* to show someone around? She barely knew the way to the restroom!

"I know you'll like her," he went on cheerfully.

Bad psychology. Everyone knew statements like that set up automatic resistance. Juli could feel hers steadily growing.

His round face took on a serious look. "At Hillcrest we pride ourselves on hosting a variety of students from other countries. This is our first from Ireland and —"

"Ireland!" Juli sat up straight. Shamrocks danced in her head, along with the setting from *Finian's Rainbow*, the play Cove had staged the year before. Great. Wasn't it enough that she'd probably been branded "Julianne" forever at her new school? Who needed an Irish immigrant hanging around her neck to make things worse than they already were?

If Mr. Smiles caught her waves of hostility, he ignored them. He bounded up from his desk, flung open a door behind him, and said with a flourish, "Julianne Scott, this is Shannon Riley."

Shannon stood just Juli's height; her weight roughly equaled Juli's trim 120 pounds. There the resemblance ended. Shannon wore her crow-black hair like a shining cap, close to her head, with bangs and a bit of swing. It contrasted sharply with Juli's shoulder length, blondish-brown waves. The stranger's lashes were long and thick. Juli's irritation trembled at the uncertainty in the gray-blue eyes, and crumbled when Shannon said with a touch of brogue, "It's good to be meetin' you."

"Me, too." Juli scrambled out of her chair. If Shannon Riley were a sample, *viva la* immigrants. Laws should be revised to welcome a whole lot more.

"Shannon hasn't registered yet," Mr. Smiles announced. "Could you help her choose? She brings the finest report of any new student except you, Julianne."

"Of course. But Mr. Smiles, would you please just call me Juli?" Realizing her slip of tongue, she cast an agonized glance at Shannon, daring her to laugh.

Shannon didn't. Mr. Smiles nodded, rubbed his hands together, gave the girls another cheerful grin, and ushered them out of his office.

"He does blather on," Shannon whispered with a wicked look in her incredible Irish eyes. "But he's a darlin' man, isn't he?"

Juli would never have called him that. She grinned, far more interested in Shannon than in the principal. "How did you happen to come here? I mean, Bellingham is a long way from Ireland." She knew she was blathering worse than Mr. Smiles but didn't know any other way to find out about the fascinating newcomer.

"A great-uncle died and left Grand, that's my grandfather Ryan Riley, some property on your Skagit River."

Juli noticed she pronounced the name of the river correctly. Sometimes radio and TV announcers who didn't know any better pronounced it "Skag-it," rather than "Scadge-it."

"Grand came to see it some time ago and loved it. I never thought he'd consider leavin' Ireland." Her eyes opened wider. "Mither died about a year ago. Father (she pronounced it fey-ther) said if Grand could find work for him, he'd come and bring me, so here we are. Father's learnin' to be a fine banker. I'm to go to school here, and Grand's runnin' the Skagit House."

"Your grandfather owns the *Skagit House?*" Juli gasped.

"For certain. Have you been there?" A smile tilted Shannon's lips.

"Never to stay, but we've driven past at least a gazillion times." Juli thought of the large, Colonial-style guest house high atop the bank at a sweeping bend of the river. A pang shot through her. "I always planned to buy it when I got rich —" *from writing mysteries,* she almost added.

"It's nay for sale, but if your folks be willin' we can stay there often." She must have taken Juli's thrilled silence for agreement because she reminded, "I must be for registerin'."

Juli recovered enough to say, "Let's try to get you into some of my classes." Shannon wound up with Juli in science, drama, an honors writing class, and orchestra. Juli told her she should play a harp instead of the flute. Shannon crossed her eyes and stuck out her tongue. "It's enough Irish I am, what with my name and speech."

Hillcrest High was so much bigger than Cove that Juli managed to get them lost three times before noon.

"It's like the blind leadin' a friend, isn't it?" Shannon asked.

"What?" Juli stopped so quickly, a boy behind her almost smashed into her. He mumbled something impolite and moved on.

"You know. The old sayin'." Shannon leaned closer and whispered, "I had a list and I've been practicin' to talk like you Yankees." Her teeth flashed in a wide smile. "When in Rome, do as the Italians do."

Juli almost asked her if Noah, as in Noah's Ark, wrote the list. Instead she said, "Uh, those are clichés and it's 'the blind leading the blind' and 'when in Rome, do as the Romans do.' "

"For sure?" Being corrected didn't seem to bother Shannon at all. "Please tell me when I'm for speakin' wrong."

Instant liking deepened into friendship, assisted by the fact that Shannon and her father bought a small, two-story brick home just a few blocks from the Scotts.

"It has to be more than coincidence," Shannon said one blue and gold October afternoon as they scuffed through brilliant leaves toward her house after school. "I mean, findin' a home we both were for likin' right here in your neighborhood."

"Coincidence, with us practically beating on doors in the neighborhood and asking if someone wanted to sell their home?" Juli scoffed.

"Then how about you gettin' picked to show me around?" Shannon persisted. "We could have been like two ships passing in the darkness, never knowin' the other sailed by."

Juli looked at the friend who had become the sister she had always wanted. "That's 'two ships that pass in the night,' not darkness." She thought of the difference Shannon's coming had made. "I — I guess God knew I needed you."

Shannon's eyes turned misty blue. "Me, too." She gave Juli a quick hug and dropped her books. Instead of picking them up, she placed her hands on her hips and did a joyous, impromptu Irish jig on the sidewalk.

"Way to go!" someone called from a passing car filled with laughing students. It didn't daunt Shannon. She merely curtsied and waved.

No amount of friendly correction changed Shannon's misquoting, that day or in the weeks and months that followed. Her speech improved and she lost much of her brogue. But she retained many of her "Rileyisms," as Hillcrest students called them. They became her trademark, like the MGM lion or Ronald McDonald, adding hilarity to school and church gatherings. Her friends caught themselves quoting Shannon. When Mr. Smiles absentmindedly repeated, "Where there's a will, there's a lawyer," everyone who heard him howled, even Juli.

Gradually, the sharp pain in Juli's heart settled to a dull ache. She and Mom had gone through grief counseling. It helped a lot just to know their feelings were normal. Juli hadn't completely abandoned the idea Dad might not be dead, but when November came with its branches stark and bare against the wintry sky, hope faded. In a couple of months it would be a whole year. If Dad were alive and coming home, he would have returned by now.

Just before Thanksgiving, Juli awakened to discover heavy fog had blotted out the morning sunshine. Murky, smokelike tendrils writhed in the air, dampening her spirits as effectively as an unexpected shower.

"I wish Mom didn't have to be a teacher," Juli told God and the too-empty house after her mother left. "I hate this gloom. Funny. Fog never bothered me when Dad was around." She blinked hard, sighed, and peered out the kitchen window. Her heart suddenly leaped to her throat. Was that — it couldn't be a lurking figure, gray as the day had become!

Dial 911! an inner voice screamed.

Juli started for the phone, her gaze riveted through the window. Nothing. She cautiously opened the door, stepped outside, and stared at the spot. Only drifting fog

44

swayed to and fro in the empty backyard.

Shaking and shaken, Juli dashed back inside, slammed and locked the door. She breathlessly leaned against it. "God, am I turning into a basket case?" She put on her fleece-lined denim jacket, locked the front door, and punched in the security code. Then she ran as if pursued by howling wolves to the bus stop.

Settle down, she told herself. *Shannon has been there for you through more than shadows in an empty yard.* It helped, but not enough.

Juli glanced back. A gray curtain completely blanketed her home, hiding whatever secrets the backyard might hold.

Chapter 4

Of all the mornings for Shannon not to be at the bus stop! She couldn't be sick or she'd have called. Her dad must have driven her to school. Why hadn't they asked Juli if she'd like a ride? Resentment shot through her. If she'd gone with them, she wouldn't have been scared half to death. Her conscience prodded her. Shannon had a right to time alone with her father. Juli sighed and climbed on the bus.

"Where's your friend?" the friendly driver wanted to know. "One of you without the other's like —"

"— ham without eggs," Juli finished and took a seat about halfway back. If she had a dollar for every time he said that she'd be rich. The famous part would come with her first published book. She laughed. This morning at breakfast she had asked, "Hey, Mom. What color BMW do you want from my first royalties?"

Anne Scott cocked one eyebrow. "Per- haps you should at least have an outline before making a down payment."

"Whatever." Juli carelessly waved her mother's suggestion away. Now she grinned. If Mom only knew! At this very moment, an idea for a story so exciting and fresh Juli believed it just might win *Seventeen*'s annual fiction contest gnawed at her brain like a mouse at a chunk of cheddar. With the ease of long practice, she slid into a daydream that lasted until the bus lurched to a stop.

"All out," the driver called.

Juli clicked her brain channel from future to present. She stepped to the curb in front of Hillcrest High and spotted Shannon running toward her, face filled with excitement. "Just wait 'til you hear what I have to tell you!"

"I have something to tell you, too. This morning I —"

"Is it more important than news about Dave Gilmore?" Shannon cut in.

The teasing question instantly grabbed Juli's attention. "What are you up to? Did I say I like Dave? I don't think so."

Shannon grinned tormentingly. She waited until they reached their first class before saying, "Too bad. Skagit House is going to be closed for minor repairs over the holidays. Grand says I can have a house party right after Christmas!"

"*Dave Gilmore* is coming?" An awful thought picked at Juli. "You didn't tell him I liked him, did you?"

"I don't think so," Shannon mimicked. "Don't you trust me? Good things come to those who are patient." Their teacher came in. "Tell you later."

"To those who *wait*," Juli hissed, wishing she could hide her feelings better. Shannon could see through her as clearly as the giant icicles that hung from the roof of Skagit House in winter. Deep down she knew Shannon wouldn't betray her, but how had she snagged Dave Gilmore for her house party?

No one could carry on a private conversation in the cafeteria, and between classes, every time Juli tried to bring up the exciting news, someone interrupted. "It's a conspiracy," she muttered when they finally boarded the bus for home.

"Conspiracy is what we need for you to impress Dave," Shannon said. "How come when a million boys are practically camping in your yard, you like the one who isn't?" She blinked. "Hey, is that it?"

Juli couldn't escape her friend's searching gaze. "Maybe." She wouldn't admit even to her best friend how much she liked Dave.

"He can't be allergic to blonds," Shannon

pointed out. "He's never all that far away from you at youth meetings or church fun nights." She cocked her head to one side. "Funny that your hair never darkened much. Girls who have to rinse would die for that mane. Especially Amy Hilton."

"Bingo." Juli smirked. "For your information, there are never more than half a million boys around at any given time. My hair is camouflage."

"I thought you wanted to know about Dave," Shannon reminded. Obviously enjoying herself, she added, "At first he didn't act interested. I just knew he was going to say no. After he found out you'd be there, though, he said it sounded great."

"Why do you always start your stories at the end?" Juli demanded. "I feel like I get the final score before I see the kickoff!"

Shannon nudged Juli with her elbow. "Did you hear me? Dave Gilmore acted like he couldn't care less about the house party until your name came up."

"I heard you. I'm just wondering exactly *how* my name came up." She fixed an accusing stare on her friend's laughing face.

"You want the truth, the whole truth, and nothing but —"

"You sound like you're swearing in a witness. Of course I do, but keep your

49

voice down," Juli warned.

"As I was saying before I was so rudely cut short —"

"Interrupted."

"I just happened to be inviting Ted and Amy Hilton and John Foster when Dave walked up."

"You invited *Amy?*" Juli couldn't believe what she was hearing.

"She has a terrific brother," Shannon said triumphantly. "There's more than one way to get what you want."

"So how did Dave Gilmore bite the dust?"

Shannon sniffed and the corners of her mouth turned down. "Even I know that sayin' went out with the Lone Ranger."

Juli gave her a little shove.

"Mercy me, do you want to hear this or don't you?"

"Yes, please." When Shannon had enough, she reverted to brogue.

Her friend eyed her suspiciously but said, "Amy started in on how terrific it was at Skagit House and how my grandfather was getting out the sleigh in case it snowed. Dave just grunted. I asked if he'd be free after Christmas. He admitted he might so I invited him to go with us." She giggled.

" 'Who's us?' he wanted to know.

"I answered, 'Juli, Mom — I call Juli's

50

mother that — Grand, Dad and me; Ted, Amy, and John. Want to come?'

"He said it sounded great and to count him in."

"You just happened to be talking with the others when Dave came along?" Juli said sarcastically, while her heart pounded in anticipation.

Shannon put on an aggrieved look. "Would I be for stagin' such a thing?"

"You don't fool me, but thanks. I owe you." Juli grinned and thought of the coming holiday. She should be able to make an impression on Dave at the Skagit House. Ted liked Shannon and John liked Amy. Juli made a face. Amy. Small and cuddly, with claws that went in or out depending on whether a boy was around. *She'd better not get her claws out for Dave. If she does, I — I'll make her the villain in my next story!* Juli vowed.

That's a real Christian thing to do, a little voice inside reminded. Juli bit her lip and mentally argued, *Christians aren't perfect. Look at Amy. Never misses church or youth meetings. Besides . . .*

Juli didn't finish the unspoken sentence. She still struggled to get back on a fully trusting basis with God. She said her prayers and talked to Him, but it wasn't the

51

same. Had her faith been so shattered when Dad didn't come home that snowy January night that she'd never get all of her trust back? She shivered and pulled her jacket closer. The thought of always feeling apart from God frightened her.

"Don't go away from me, Juli," Shannon's low voice pleaded.

"Huh? Oh. Sorry."

"I understand." Her enormous, black-fringed eyes showed she did.

Juli didn't want to talk about it, especially now, when Shannon had gone to so much trouble to do something nice. "Isn't closing the Skagit House going to cut Grand out of a lot of business?" she asked. "It's always so crammed, especially over the holidays."

"Predictions are for a cold, hard winter," Shannon began. "Several regulars canceled, so Grand's closing December 24 and won't open again until January 2. He says he wants an old-fashioned family Christmas. The Scotts are part of the family, you know." She patted Juli's arm. "Besides, by the time Grand pays the help extra as he always does on holidays, plus heats the whole place, profits aren't that great. We want you and Mom for the entire vacation. The others can come on the 26th." Her warm smile spread over her excited face. "It's so neat that

Mom's teaching, instead of being on a job where she couldn't get time off."

Juli swallowed hard. "I was wondering how we'd make it through Christmas."

Shannon's sparkle dimmed. "Once you face up to something, it's never so hard again. Dad and I found that out when Mother died." Her eyes grew misty. Even with Juli, she rarely opened up this much. "It also helps a lot to break the pattern, especially at holidays. Dad and I did that last year, by going to Scotland. You'll be better off at Skagit House than in Bellingham."

"Right." Juli grabbed her backpack and followed Shannon down the aisle when the bus stopped.

"Good to see you together," the friendly driver told them. "One of you without the other's like —"

"— ham without eggs," the girls chorused.

"Be careful," he warned. "The fog's rolling in off the bay again."

"We will." The girls stepped down from the bus into a world of gray. Busy talking, neither noticed how dark it had grown, although still mid-afternoon.

"I'll come help you make dinner so I can ask Mom about Christmas," Shannon plotted. "Or would she prefer an engraved invitation?" She stuck her nose in the air and droned, "The Rileys request the pleasure of your presence at a Christmas house party. RSVP."

"Request the pleasure of your company," Juli corrected.

"It's not your *company* we're for invitin'," Shannon haughtily informed her. "It's you and Mom."

Juli laughed, but when they reached the Scott home, she stopped abruptly on the front walk. "Would you believe I never told you what happened this morning?"

"I believe it." Shannon laughed. It sounded hollow in the foggy air. "Once you heard the name Dave Gilmore you forgot everything else. So what happened?"

Juli glanced toward the backyard, but couldn't penetrate the smothering curtain. "I thought I saw someone." She felt foolish saying it out loud. "When I looked again, nothing was there. Probably just the fog."

"Probably," Shannon agreed. "It can play tricks and make you think all kinds of things. What's for dinner?"

"Spaghetti pie, tossed salad, garlic bread, and fresh fruit. Mom says we'll have enough junk food during the holidays, so we're trying to eat well now to make up for it." Juli unlocked the door and led the way to the kitchen. "Pull the shades and turn on the lights, will you? A day like this is creepy." She didn't add it was also a perfect day to hide anyone who might be lurking in the yard.

Stop it, she mentally ordered herself. *Shannon's right. Fog can play tricks with your eyes. The same things are in the yard that are always there: trees and shrubs; flower beds and vegetable garden, dormant now; a padlocked storage shed. No table or lawn chairs or awning — they go back out in the spring.* She tossed her jacket on a chair and got busy making the spaghetti pie. Shannon worked on the salad, as familiar in the Scott kitchen as in her own.

Mom came home to a warm, spicy welcome. "Hi, daughter and second daughter." Anne shook moisture from her hair and yawned. "What a day!" She sank into a chair. "It gets dark so early this time of year, especially with the fog rolling in from the bay. I'll run you home after we eat, Shannon. Or is your dad coming for you?"

"It isn't that far," Shannon protested. "I can walk."

"We won't take chances." Mom sniffed. "Fee fie foe fum, I smell spaghetti pie, yum yum." She opened the oven and peeked in.

Shannon giggled appreciatively but Juli

told her mother, "It's obvious from whom I did *not* get my writing talent. That was absolutely awful. We'll be ready to eat by the time you change."

"Your wish is my command." Mom bowed low and started out of the kitchen.

"Wait!" Shannon quickly explained about the house party. Mom's face lit up like the Fourth of July. She hugged Juli and Shannon before hurrying across the dining room and down the hall without a trace of fatigue.

"She acts like she just won the lottery," Juli commented, secretly glad to see laughter in Mom's face. She hated the exhaustion Mom couldn't always hide at the end of her busy days.

Shannon raised silky brows. "Of course. After all, how many people get to spend Christmas at Skagit House?"

Juli felt more carefree and lighthearted than she had in weeks. "Let me see." She counted on her fingers. "You and I and . . ."

"For this I gave up going straight home and studying?" Shannon stated, keeping a straight face when Juli knew she was dying to laugh. "Just for that I get seconds on everything."

By the time they finished eating, the unpredictable November weather had changed.

A chill wind Mom said felt like snow dispersed the fog. Some of the heavy clouds scudded away, leaving great patches of clear sky and a slice of moon. "Let's walk Shannon home," Juli suggested.

"Good idea," Mom approved. "I need the exercise and it's only six o' clock. We'll have to bundle up, though. That breeze is straight off the bay."

Juli shoved a baseball cap over her hair. Shannon turned up the hood on her coat. Mom grabbed a long wool scarf. They covered the few blocks between the houses in record time. Juli liked the brick house where Sean Riley and his daughter lived. It had many-paned windows and a carved front door. Shannon often complained about how long it took to wash the windows, but Juli knew she didn't really mind. Besides, the Rileys had a cleaning woman come in weekly for the heavy stuff. Shannon did the rest.

"Thanks for bringing her home. Do you have time to come in?" Sean called from the open doorway. Light streamed out and silhouetted the tall, imposing banker who strongly resembled his daughter.

"Not tonight." Mom sighed. "I have phone calls to make about the upcoming school bond levy. Sometimes I wish teachers could just teach."

"See you tomorrow, Juli." Shannon opened the wrought iron gate and ran to the house. The Scotts shivered, called good-night, and hurried toward home.

Chapter 5

"In a few months Shannon and I will have our driver's licenses." Juli skipped a little. "Sean and Grand may get her a car. Not new, of course." She hastily added, "Isn't that great?" Mom's salary wouldn't stretch for a second car.

"It's great you can be glad and not envious." Mom quickened her pace. "Brrr. We may get snow tonight."

"I hope so. And I don't need a car with Shannon so close." Juli gave her mother a quick hug and shut her lips tight to hold back a humongous secret. Far better to surprise Mom by winning this year's *Seventeen* fiction contest than to just announce she planned to enter. Her feet barely touched the sidewalk. One sale would lead to another, then another, until someday . . .

"Ow!" Juli stumbled over a rough place in the sidewalk and clutched at her mother. So much for walking on air. She limped her way home, glad Dave Gilmore hadn't been there to see her near swan dive. What if she had broken a toe with only a few weeks remaining before Christmas vacation!

Once inside, Juli yanked off her shoe and wiggled her toes. Instant relief. One ached a bit, but none was broken. She did her homework under Clue's watchful eyes, forcing herself to ignore the rising wind that tore around the corners of the house and whistled through tall rhododendrons outside the windows.

"Almost finished?" Mom asked as she appeared in the bedroom doorway.

"As much as I can be without more reference material." Juli banged a book shut. "Get your calls made?"

"Yes, if talking to nine answering machines out of seventeen calls counts."

She yawned and gave Juli a hug. "It's bedtime for me. See you tomorrow."

Juli hugged her back and gave a little bounce. "Right." After Mom left, she grabbed Clue and whispered, "I can hardly wait! Tomorrow we'll talk about the house party." She pictured Dave Gilmore, and her heart beat a little faster. "We also get to read our stories in the honors writing class." She grinned. "I wonder what Mrs. Sorenson will say? And Shannon. I think it's my best yet." She hit instant replay in her brain and brought up the day they had received instructions.

"Write anything you wish," Mrs. Sorenson had said. "Things that come from deep inside you, the well from which all good creative writing springs."

Juli had been ecstatic. "It's my favorite kind of assignment," she told Shannon on their way home. "What are you going to write?"

Shannon's Irish eyes sparkled. "A story of how the potato crop failed in Ireland in the mid-1800s and the famine that followed."

Juli stared at her. "Where's your sense of romance? History is about as creative as that thing." She pointed to a mottled slug hunched on the sidewalk.

Shannon smiled mysteriously. "Wait and see. What about your assignment?"

Juli felt her cheeks burn and knew her eyes got shiny, the way they always did when she thought of her someday-success as an author. "I don't know yet. There are so many things! Maybe a romantic adventure in Tanganyika . . ."

Shannon wrinkled her smooth forehead. "Is there still a Tanganyika? The way they keep changing the names of countries, you might —"

"Will you just listen? That's only one idea, and of course I'll look up Tanganyika or whatever before I hand it in." Another idea exploded in her brain. "I know. I'll have a sinister stranger follow a high school sophomore."

"In a brown UPS van?" Shannon giggled and pointed across the foggy street. "Remember when you got so paranoid about them? Everywhere we went you noticed brown delivery trucks."

Juli set her lips in a straight line. "You have to admit there are a lot of them. It seems to me we see a whole bunch more than we should. Maybe someone really is following us and disguising himself as a UPS driver." Shivers crawled up her spine until the van took off down the street without a backward glance from the obviously bored driver.

"Why don't you write about something you know?" Shannon asked.

"No way do authors only write about things they've experienced."

Shannon's eyes twinkled. "That's good, 'cause for someone who wants to write romances, you aren't getting much practical experience!"

"So? I like being kissed, but only by the right person. Besides, I don't see you going out with octopus types."

"You won't, either." Shannon tossed her

dark head. "My folks had such a good thing in their marriage; I don't intend to get involved and spoil my future. Anyway, God expects us to stay pure."

"Someone should remind Amy Hilton of that. Have you noticed the way she stands as close as she can to a boy and gazes up into his face as if he were the greatest and only person in the world?"

"Meow." Shannon twirled imaginary cat whiskers.

Juli couldn't help laughing. No matter how serious a conversation they had, Shannon could get to her every time.

Juli wasn't laughing after Shannon read her story titled "Katie" in class. Instead of just giving facts, Shannon had created a teenage heroine to represent all the starving people in Ireland. She crawled inside Katie and showed it through her eyes: Hunger. Failing crops. The loss of family members. The miserable ships called *coffin boats* on which those who escaped sickness and starvation came to America. Katie's feelings when she first set foot on American soil, and the thankfulness in her heart. Shannon ended with Katie saying to a younger sister, "Don't fret, darlin'. Tomorrow will be for bringin' us better things."

For a moment no one clapped. Juli

reached for a tissue, so proud she wondered if she would burst. She saw Dave Gilmore pass a hand over his eyes, as if to wipe away something in them. Then the class went wild. It took a long time for them to settle down, enough for Juli to panic. She was alphabetically next in line to read. How could she stand before the class after this? The story she had worked on so hard, the "masterpiece" she'd felt might be a contest winner, crumbled to worthlessness when compared with the touching tale whose poignant echoes still filled the classroom.

"Juli?" Mrs. Sorenson's hazel eyes shone. Juli could tell how impressed she'd been with Shannon's assignment. "I know Shannon's story is a hard act to follow, but you always come through for us."

If only the floor would open and swallow me and my story, she thought. But it didn't. Juli started to get up, then sank back into her seat. "Do I *have* to read?" she blurted out.

The whole class became quiet. Mrs. Sorenson looked surprised. "Of course. You know the rules. Everyone reads and learns from the in-class critiquing done according to the guidelines set up at the beginning of the year."

Why hadn't she listened to Shannon and written something she knew? It was too late now. All Juli could do was hope the story didn't sound as trite as she suddenly recognized it was. So far, she had a four-point average in class, along with Shannon. Now a sickening feeling told her she was going down in one big *splat.*

Her footsteps sounded loud in her ears. Mrs. Sorenson blurred before her eyes. She reached the front of the room, took a deep breath, and started reading. Was that actually Juli Scott, the star debater, mouthing overused phrases and unconvincing happenings? Her bulky pink knit sweater that looked so great when she put it on that morning felt heavy and dull, as heavy and dull as she knew her story sounded compared to Shannon's. A spatter of polite applause led by Shannon followed. Juli knew it was for her as a friend, definitely not for her story. She handed it to Mrs. Sorenson and stumbled back to her desk.

"Who has a comment for Juli?" Mrs. Sorenson's voice reflected the same disappointment Juli felt in herself. She stared at her fingers, clenched so tightly they showed white at the knuckles. Her first real chance to be creative and she'd blown it. She should have gone with a "slug" story.

Please. Make them be kind. Juli clenched her teeth. Then deliverance. A miracle, right there in good old Hillcrest High. Everyone else thought it was just the bell signaling the end of the period. Juli knew better. The ringing sound offered reprieve at dawn, pardon one minute before midnight, all the last-ditch rescues ever globbed into one terrific moment on TV.

Mrs. Sorenson raised her voice over the chatter. "Juli, I'd like to see you."

Shannon raised sympathetic eyebrows and mouthed, "Meet you outside." Juli wished Shannon had given her a Rileyism. She had a feeling she was going to need it.

Mrs. Sorenson didn't waste a minute, once the classroom cleared. "I hope you learned a lesson today. I can't give you more than a C on your story. Juli, you have tremendous natural ability, but are cluttering it up with a bunch of garbage." She riffled the pages of "Last Dance" and etched a heavy red line through a sentence.

Juli cringed. "The late evening silence broken only by rhythmic, murmurous waves gently caressing the sand" had been a favorite.

"Contrast this with Shannon's opening sentence," Mrs. Sorenson quietly said. " 'Katie was hungry. Again.' Both tell us something, but how much?"

Juli saw what she meant. "I tried to paint a

word picture. Shannon hooked readers with the single word 'again.' No one could stop there."

Mrs. Sorenson leaned back in her chair and looked at her seriously. "Shannon does not write better than you, Juli. Her advantage comes from writing what she knows."

Depression hit Juli like a firebomb. "Who would want to read about my life?" she cried. "How can I write interesting things when I'm so ordinary?"

"You are far from ordinary," Mrs. Sorenson protested. "Search out the things you believe and want and see and feel. Your best work so far was a short piece on the Skagit House. It contained too many adjectives and adverbs instead of strong verb-and-noun description, but had charm and warmth from your feelings. This is what Shannon did with 'Katie.' She explored her own feelings of fear and discouragement, then transferred them to her heroine."

Twenty minutes later Juli left the classroom, torn between wondering if she could ever write anything worth reading and Mrs. Sorenson's parting challenge:

"When I see potential in students, I demand their best. I intend to be harder on you and Shannon than the other students in class. I know what you can do if you try.

67

You've never come right out and said you hope to one day become a professional author. I'm not asking you to say it now, either, except to yourself. The odds against making it are terrific, as you know." Her eyes glistened. "Yet if you believe in yourself and vow never to quit, I have no doubt that someday I will see the name *Juli Scott* on a book cover." She tapped the offensive manuscript with a scornful finger. "It won't be from writing this kind of stuff." She marked a huge red C on "Last Dance" and handed it back.

Shannon patiently waited by their lockers. "Well?"

"Rejection slips will never wipe me out after this," Juli told her. "She flattened me, but good." She opened her locker and grabbed at a pile of sliding books.

"So how come you look like the cat that ate the parakeet?" Shannon inquired.

"Not parakeet, canary!" Juli laughed. "Mrs. Sorenson told me if I wanted it badly enough, I could become an author. And she should know." Mrs. Sorenson was also known as "Allison Terrence," *the* Allison Terrence whose first novel had recently hit the market and was receiving favorable reviews. Juli knew it had taken her teacher ten years and some 500 rejection slips to become a published author!

Juli gasped. If it took *her* that long, she'd be through college, maybe even married.

Mrs. Sorenson mercifully didn't refer to "Last Dance" again. Neither did the class. The next assignment was to interview an unusual, important, or unique person. Juli picked Mom, who promptly disagreed.

"You'd get too emotional," she warned. "Don't choose Shannon, for the same reason. When's the interview due?"

"Second week in January. Why?" Juli sprawled on the rug in front of the fireplace, one of her favorite places in the whole world. Something about those leaping, tumbling, dancing flames fascinated her. *Although,* she sourly told herself, *Mrs. Sorenson would red ink out all my great adjectives!*

"Why not interview Shannon's grandfather, Ryan Riley?" Mom suggested. She hesitated between a scarlet and a sapphire bow for the Christmas package she was wrapping. Anne Scott always bought items ahead of time and on sale. Juli usually dashed out the week before Christmas and couldn't find what she wanted. Now the firelight reflected on the silver paper and cast a glow on Mom's face.

"Good idea. Hey, you're a lot prettier now." When Mom glanced up, Juli felt dumb. "Uh, I mean, your face isn't so thin and your eyes have lost some of their worry."

Anne perked the loops of the red bow and dropped the package to the rug. "Life does go on, Juli. There are still times when I miss your father so much it's almost unbearable, but I know he wouldn't want us to grieve forever." A bright drop fell and she hastily brushed it away.

Juli just sat there wondering for the thousandth time why God had let Dad die in the first place.

"It's nice you're growing up." Mom smiled. "I can talk with you on an adult level. Not that I expect you to become the parent, as some widows do."

Juli grunted and shifted to a more comfortable position. "Fat chance."

"Let's just say a daughter like you has made the difference. Without you and God . . ." Her voice trailed off. Juli felt either Mom had grown younger or she, Juli, had become older. It gave her a bittersweet feeling. For a single moment, she longed to seize the peaceful evening and hold it close. Instead, she changed the subject.

"Want to hear Shannon's latest Riley-ism?"

"Sure." Mom's grin returned.

"We were talking about Ireland. She said it was very green in spring and I told her Mrs. Sorenson would cut out the very because it weakens otherwise strong writing by calling attention to itself. Shannon stuck her nose in the air and informed me, 'she who laughs last, laughs hardest,' instead of 'laughs best.' "

Mom chuckled and Juli added, "She also said I might be her best friend but it wouldn't keep her from trying to beat me out of first place whenever she could. I don't mind. Friendly competition gives us both a reason to work harder." She yawned. "Want a soda? I'm really dry." By the time Mom called "No thanks," Juli was halfway to the kitchen. Darkness had fallen, so she reached to close the mini-blinds beneath the blue curtains.

Her hand froze in midair. A tall, thin shadow stretched across the back lawn, grotesque and terrifying.

Chapter 6

The shadow moved. Blind, unreasoning terror swept through Juli, surging like the Skagit River in flood. She yanked the mini-blinds closed and screamed, "Mom, come quick! There's someone in our backyard!"

Mom ran into the kitchen. "Are you sure?"

"Yes." Juli knew she was babbling but couldn't stop. "A — a shadow." She turned off the light and cautiously reopened the blinds. "It was . . ." her eyes widened. The tall, thin shadow had vanished. "It's gone!" She whirled to face her mother. "Someone was there. I know it!"

"Maybe it was a shadow from one of the trees," Mom told her. She looked out. "There's nothing there now." She closed the blinds again and snapped on the kitchen light. "Do you want me to call the police?"

Juli sagged against the door, holding on to the knob for support. "What good would it do?" she asked bitterly. "An empty yard doesn't hold much of a threat. They'd think

I was seeing things." *Just like the other time,* a little voice whispered inside her. She opened her mouth to tell Mom and thought better of it. She had no proof of a prowler, either then or now.

"I'll get up early and check for tracks," she told Clue just before she turned out her light. "I'll take Polaroid pictures of them, so I'll have proof."

Hours later she awakened from a nightmare, groaning and soaked with sweat. For a long time she lay still, afraid to open her eyes. When she did, the dim light of a snowy morning sneaked in her window and showed her peaceful room. Everything was as it should be, even the Levi's she'd been too tired to hang up the night before and her Nikes upside down near them. She slid from bed and tiptoed to the window. So much for getting clues. Enough fresh snow blanketed the backyard to cover tracks made by anything smaller than a herd of elephants.

Juli hurried back to bed, grabbed Clue, and hugged him. "It was only a dream," she whispered. Yet every detail remained clear. She'd been at the Skagit House in autumn. Golden leaves fell into gloriously colored piles. The tang of wood smoke hung in the air.

Soon the leaves became snowflakes. Fir

73

trees showed dark against white-clad fields and distant hills. Two laughing girls tossed snowballs and shared hopes for the future. Shadows from slowly moving branches reflected in the Skagit River, making ever-changing patterns.

The dream changed. Juli stood on the riverbank. Where had the friendly river she loved gone? A greedy brown monster writhed its way closer and closer to where she stood. To her horror, the flood gobbled inch after inch of the beautiful Skagit House grounds. She turned to flee — and froze. A brown UPS van sat half-hidden by a clump of white birches.

Shannon's voice came from a distance. "Don't be paranoid." It didn't stop the fear that overwhelmed Juli. She tried to pray, but no words came. Then she saw it. A shadowy figure, halfway between her and the van. The dream ended there.

Juli lay rigid until she heard Mom get up. She headed for the shower. Why would she dream such a thing? She let the warm water wash over her until Mom finally called and said she'd be late if she didn't hurry. The very normality of the day calmed her jangled nerves. Breakfast with Mom. Talk about the vacation at Skagit House. Meeting Shannon at the bus stop.

"Hey, Juli, here comes your friend." Shannon pointed at a brown UPS van.

Juli felt the blood drain from her face. She opened her mouth to describe her dream about the van and the shadowy figure but decided against it. Talking about it even with Shannon meant making it more real. Nothing must ever disturb her feelings of peace and safety centered around the Skagit House. Before Dad died, Juli knew her security came from God. Since then, she'd felt so let down she couldn't talk with Him without feeling angry and hurt. It made her wonder if God still had control over her world.

I know You still love me, her heart said. *It's just that* — she couldn't continue.

"Hey, are you all right?" Shannon swung back toward Juli, her face concerned under the hood of her parka. Juli knew without being told how often Shannon realized when she was troubled. And that it saddened her friend when Juli endured church instead of being blessed the way she used to be — and Shannon still was. A few times she had sent little cards with a "God-loves-you, this-too-shall-pass" message. They didn't melt the ice that encased Juli's heart, and they never discussed them. Neither did they answer the question, "Why, God?" any better than Mom or the pastor had been able to months earlier.

"Come back, come back, wherever you are," Shannon teased, although the little worried look remained. "I want to talk about our house party. You have to work for your room and board, you know."

Shannon's statement acted like rain on sidewalk chalk art. "Work! Who said anything about work? What is this, a slave auction?"

"Everyone works at Skagit House when the staff goes on holiday." Shannon cocked her head and grinned mischievously. "Can't you just see Dave Gilmore in cap and apron dusting the whatnots and pictures of who's-its?"

"It's easier to see him in a ski suit shoveling paths and packing in wood." Anticipation chased some of the chill from Juli's veins. "I suppose we'll be cooking, too. It's not up to your dad or Grand or you to do all the work."

"Not Mom, either. Everyone helps at this house party."

"Everyone? Amy won't get excited about washing dishes."

"We have a dishwasher. Of course, there are always bathrooms to clean." Pure mischief danced in Shannon's eyes. "I wonder if I can figure out a way to make sure Amy gets the duty slips marked 'bathrooms' when we draw for jobs?"

Suddenly Juli felt gloriously happy. "I don't really care. This is going to be the best vacation ever, and I won't let anything — including Amy or cleaning bathrooms — spoil it."

"Right." Shannon did a little dance on the snow-covered sidewalk.

"Besides," Juli mumbled to herself after they reached school and parted for their first class, "if someone in a UPS van is following me, which of course is ridiculous, he wouldn't find me at Skagit House in a million years." The thought comforted her for the next few days. She saw no more evidence of prowlers, and any UPS van that passed did just that — passed on by.

"Sledding tonight?" Dave Gilmore called to Juli in the hall that afternoon.

"Yup. Sledding tonight." She gave a thumbs-up sign, feeling glad the Bellingham police had barricaded off some of the quieter streets for coasting. There was nothing like belly flopping on a sled and racing downhill! Juli had feared when she grew up no one would go with her. She laughed. Shannon fixed that by appearing at Juli's with a brand new sled after the first snowfall. They'd had a blast. The next day they told everyone at school what fun it was. That same night, a dozen boys and a half-dozen girls showed up, some with sleds as new-looking as Shannon's.

That evening Dave Gilmore's blue ski jacket just matched his eyes. His blond hair hung out of an alpine-looking hat. If Juli hadn't caught Shannon making signals behind Dave's back, Juli wouldn't have known she was practically drooling. She smothered a laugh. "I can't wait to get to Skagit House."

"Yes!" His right arm shot into the air. "You're going early, aren't you?"

"Shannon's father is driving Mom and Shannon and me up the morning of the 24th." She took in a breath of sheer excitement. "Funny how wrong you can be about bankers. I used to think they only worked the hours the bank stayed open. Mr. Riley puts in really long hours."

Laugh crinkles appeared at the corner of Dave's eyes and mouth. "Anything worth doing is worth doing swell," he teased.

Juli groaned. "That's a Rileyism even Shannon hasn't used so far."

"She will." Dave struck a pose with one hand over his eyes. He gazed into the distance as if listening to faraway voices. "Methinks —"

"Methinks! You sound like Mrs. Sorenson quoting Shakespeare or someone."

Dave responded by washing her face with a handful of soft snow.

Juli didn't really care, but snatched a fistful, formed a snowball, and threw it at his back. "Come back and fight, you coward."

"Temper, temper," Dave tossed over his shoulder. His white teeth gleamed in his laughing face until Juli felt her heart beat faster. She also had the last laugh; he tripped over a plastic dishpan some kids had been using for a sled and sprawled full-length in a snow bank.

"Mighty basketball player not very light on feet," Juli taunted.

Dave sat up and grinned at her. "Speaking of mighty ballplayers, are you coming to see us waste Mount Vernon tomorrow night?"

Juli's heart thumped even harder. "How could I resist, with such a graceful forward as you on the first string?" She didn't trust herself to look at him again and felt relieved when Shannon's red-hooded head appeared from behind a tree. "Dave's practicing calisthenics in the snow so he can play ball better."

"The proof of the pudding is in the empty dish," she retorted.

Juli burst into laughter and Dave rolled in

the snow. Shannon stuck her chin in the air and loftily informed them, "Just wait 'til I get you to Ireland. We'll see how funny you sound." Juli knew she wasn't mad. Shannon always said, "Grand says people can never laugh at you if you laugh first. They can only laugh *with* you." Juli admitted it worked, at least most of the time. When Amy Hilton was around, she felt more like spitting and snarling. Juli comforted herself with the thought that even though Christians were supposed to love everyone, nothing had been said about having to *like* girls such as Amy!

The next night in the cheering section she whispered to Shannon, "Amy is so phony. She sure knows how to take advantage of being a cheerleader." Juli glared at the petite blond in the short white skirt and sapphire sweater who clung to Dave Gilmore's arm and smiled up into his face.

"He doesn't seem all that impressed," Shannon commented. Just then Dave freed himself, glanced into the stands, and smiled at the girls. He clasped both hands over his head in a victory sign and trotted onto the floor for warm-up.

"He's never done that before." Shannon's eyes twinkled. "Some people certainly do make good use of their sledding."

Juli blushed and squirmed, and changed the subject. "I sure hope we win. Mount Vernon's tough."

"No use crying before the milk's spilled, is there?"

Juli ignored her Rileyism and watched the centers tip off. Straight to Ted, then Dave. Down the floor, the Pirates handling the ball in their best style. *Swish*. The Hillcrest crowd roared. Back the other way. Loud groans when Mount Vernon scored. "They're here to *play*," Juli shouted. The game seesawed with the regularity of a tennis match. At halftime, the score stood at 39–39 and Juli felt worn out. Hillcrest's drill team marched onto the floor, sapphire and white outfits swinging in their precision drill. The cheerleaders did their stuff.

"Much as I hate to admit it, Amy's good," Juli said after Amy executed a perfect cheer and ended with a cartwheel and splits.

"Twinship fits Ted better than it does her." Shannon looked pleased when the player she admired sent a big grin toward her. "Everyone knows Amy thinks being a twin is bor-r-ring. Ted's a lot prouder of her than she deserves."

Third quarter ended in tragedy. John Foster, a terrific guard, fell hard and left the court limping. Mount Vernon slam-dunked the ball, intercepted a pass, and scored again just as time ran out. The final quarter ticked off with the Pirates just a few points behind. With three minutes to go, the score 68–65, Coach Barrett signaled for a time-out. The sweaty players huddled, listened, and charged back onto the floor.

The pass went to Dave, then across to Ted, who faked a shot, and back to Dave. *Swish.* Hillcrest scored again — 68–67. Mount Vernon got the ball and stalled. "Steal, Pirates, steal!" the fans chanted. Juli felt her fingernails dig into her hands. "Why don't they *do* something?" she cried. "Do they think we're ahead?"

Coach Barrett stood statue-like, crouched and tense. At thirty seconds the puzzled-looking Mount Vernon center fired the ball toward their star forward. He checked the clock, dribbled, and leaped into the air for a long shot. Dave had the ball the moment it left his hands. A thunderous roar rose when he headed toward the home court. Twenty seconds. Why didn't he shoot? Dave glanced at the clock and passed to Ted.

"Oh, no!" Shannon protested. "It's instant replay!"

It was. The pass to Ted. The quick sighting. The up-in-the-air that meant a faked shot. Before Ted left the floor, the Mount

Vernon squad turned toward Dave. Juli's heart sank. Ted could never get the ball through that cluster of sweaty bodies. She couldn't stand to watch. She couldn't stand not to watch, either. Frozen, she heard the countdown start. "Four. Three. Two. One."

Like a homing pigeon, Ted's long shot dropped through the basket.

"He never meant to pass back to Dave," Juli screamed above the crowd that had gone wild. "They just wanted Mount Vernon to think he would!"

"All's well that ends with our winning," Shannon yelled back. They leaped down the bleachers and onto the floor with several hundred shouting, happy fans. Juli hugged everyone she came to, even Amy, who for once proudly gave her twin brother credit. Juli caught Dave's broad grin across the crowd and his ". . . worth doing swell" floated her way.

"Ted and Dave are giving us a ride home," Shannon said in her ear. "We're supposed to wait for them in the hall outside the locker room."

"All right!" Juli frantically fished a comb from her jacket pocket and made repairs. Even Amy's gushing about how *magnificent* the team was and how *terrific* it was being related to a star couldn't dim her excitement. *Had Dave asked Ted to fix things up?* The thought stretched Juli's smile even wider.

The locker room door opened. Ted, John, and Dave came out. John limped and wore a bandage on his ankle.

"How'd you like the game?" Dave's blue eyes twinkled.

"Not bad, methinks." Juli laughed.

"Ted, I have to go home with you," Amy pouted. "The coach is taking John."

For once Ted sounded as if he wished he'd been born an only child. "No way. I'm going with Dave, Juli, and Shannon."

"I'm sure they won't mind." Amy pasted on her famous smile. "It's not like it's a date or anything, is it?" She turned to Dave.

"Not now," Ted spit out. "It might have been, without you."

"On a weeknight during training?" She raised silky eyebrows. "You have to be in early."

"I guess you're right." He sounded wiped out. "Is it okay, Dave?"

Juli's heart had bounced at the word *date*, fallen to her boots when Amy butted in. Now she gritted her teeth and numbly waited for Dave's answer.

Chapter 7

Dave grunted. "Let's go." He led the way to his '68 Mustang, held the passenger door open, and shoved the bucket seat forward.

Amy chirped, "I have to ride in the front. I get carsick in the backseat."

Was she for real? Juli doubted it, but Ted admitted, "She really does."

"You'll have to sit in front and hold her," Dave said. "Hope the police don't cite me for Amy not wearing a seat belt."

"Just what we need," Ted muttered. Shannon and Juli silently crawled into the back, but Amy chattered nonstop. Shannon looked at Juli, rolling her eyes.

Dave dropped off the Hiltons and casually asked Juli to move up front so she and Shannon would be more comfortable. She scrambled out, ignored Amy's glare, and got into the front seat.

"I'm staying at Juli's," Shannon told Dave when they started again.

Dave nodded. "So, you liked the game?" They discussed it all the way home. He waited until they reached the porch, called "See you," and drove off. They watched the Mustang's red taillights disappear, then Shannon burst out, "Can you believe Amy Hilton?"

Juli waited until they were in her bedroom with the door closed. Mom hadn't been feeling well and her bedroom lights were out. "Just think, we get two whole weeks of her. Mercy me," she mimicked. "I can hardly wait."

"Excuse me? How come you're for bein' so cheerful?" Some of Shannon's anger died, but the mixing of slang and brogue showed she was still upset.

"It doesn't make sense, does it?" Juli laughed. "Maybe because Dave and Ted didn't act one bit glad she butted in and talked all the way to her house."

"I don't see how Ted can be so nice when his sister's such a brat."

"Neither does half the student body. Even the kids who think Amy's so cool and elect her to stuff know Ted's a lot nicer person. I also have the feeling Ted thinks someone else around here is super cool."

Shannon's eyes sparkled. "He's weakening. The house party will do it. Just two more days until the holidays, and tomorrow night's our church caroling party."

"Thanks to you. I'm glad when our youth group talked about our usual name drawing for gifts you suggested Project People instead. Pastor Johnson came up with six low-income older persons who don't have families. Can you imagine? At least I still have Mom and you have Grand and your dad." Juli's voice shook.

"We have each other, too," Shannon softly reminded. She brushed away a glitter of tears. "Pastor and Mrs. Johnson matched what we contributed. It means warm sweaters and special food for people who can't afford to buy for themselves. Mrs. Johnson said she guessed sizes, but is keeping all the tags so she can exchange anything that doesn't fit." She slid into the twin bed that matched Juli's and yawned. "I feel like *I* played the basketball game!"

Juli crawled into her own bed and snapped off the light. "I know what you mean. Wonder what Amy will pull next?"

"Why not wait and see instead of trying to figure it out ahead of time?" She sounded sleepy. In a few minutes, her soft breathing showed she'd fallen asleep.

Juli closed her eyes but was so wired she slipped from bed a half hour later. Warm milk always relaxed her. Taking care not to disturb Shannon, she inched across the bedroom, down the hall, and into the kitchen. No need to turn on the light. She knew the position of all the furniture so well that the semi-darkness held no obstacles for her. Besides, some light always crept in around curtains and blinds.

While the milk warmed, Juli grew aware of the stillness outside. The storm must have stopped. She lifted the side of the mini-blinds and glanced out. The back porch light faithfully showed a well-covered ground, but no flakes in the air. A lopsided moon made the yard look like a Christmas card. How beautiful.

A heartbeat later, something moved. Juli clenched the blinds with icy fingers. Moonlight and porchlight shone on a man standing against a tall, snow-covered spruce. A gray man. Gray hair. Shabby gray coat. He seemed familiar, but from where? Why did he just stand there, staring at the kitchen door? Juli tried to call Mom and Shannon. Nothing came from her tight throat. She couldn't move.

A hissing sound behind Juli freed her from her daze. She whipped around, grabbed the pan of milk which was starting to boil over, and ran to the sink. In less than a minute, she was back at the window peeking around the blind.

The gray man had vanished, like ghostly shadows at dawn. Juli couldn't tell if there were footprints in the snow. "Don't be dumb," she fiercely told herself. "Of course there are!" Did she dare take the risk of stepping outside to find out?

"I don't think so," Juli whispered. "I'm not a coward, but I'm not stupid, either." Shivering more from fear than cold, she let the blind down and cooled the boiling milk with some from the refrigerator. The warm drink helped, but after she carefully washed the pan and got back to bed, fear rumbled through her like aftershocks from an earthquake. She held Clue tightly, her mind racing. If she could only figure out why the gray man looked familiar! Concentrating did no good. Not until she slipped into the never-never land between waking and sleeping did recognition hit, with the force of a gale sweeping in from Bellingham Bay.

Juli burrowed deeper into her bed. The gray man in the yard was the same as the mysterious man in her nightmare. She could picture him between her and the UPS van, screened by white birches near the bank of a flooding Skagit River.

If only she'd been able to call out. If only the milk hadn't boiled over. Juli pushed her face into her pillow and prayed, "God, why can't someone else see him, too? Am I imagining things? Losing it? Please, God, I need Your help." She fell asleep at last, hanging onto Clue and repeating, "Help me," over and over.

She woke early, threw on a warm robe and stepped into boots, and went out. More snow had fallen, again hiding any tracks made the night before. *Now what?* she wondered all through breakfast and on the way to the bus stop.

"Something wrong?" Shannon asked. "Or does the prospect of seeing Dave Gilmore and going caroling leave you speechless?"

She couldn't hold it in any longer. After boarding the bus, Juli told Shannon everything, keeping her voice to a whisper. Her fingers clenched inside her heavy mittens. Would her friend believe her?

"Why haven't you told Mom?" Shannon demanded. No trace of disbelief showed in her concerned face. "Or my father? Or the police?"

"The gray man is there and then he isn't." Juli stared at her hands. "It doesn't make sense. How could I dream up a gray man and then have him appear in my yard? Do you think I'm headed for the funny farm?"

"Are you kidding? You're as normal as I am, if that's any comfort." Shannon put her gloved hand over Juli's arm. "If you say you saw a gray man, you saw a gray man. Sooner or after a while someone else will see him too."

Her friend's emphatic affirmation of her healthy mental state made Juli feel a hundred percent better. "Thanks, but it's 'sooner or later,' not 'after a while.' "

Shannon waved the correction aside. "Same thing. Now, about tonight . . ."

They spent the rest of the ride wondering how many carolers would show up, especially if it snowed again.

It didn't. Brilliant winter stars and a misshapen moon brightened the cold world. Juli went from joy to disappointment when Ted showed up without Amy and said Dave wouldn't be coming either. "His folks were unexpectedly called out of town, too late to get a sitter for Dave's little sister," Ted explained.

"How about you caroling with me, Juli?" John Foster quickly put in.

"Sure." She liked the quiet boy who never missed youth activities. "Too bad Amy didn't make it," she commented when they climbed from his car and stood outside the first place they planned to carol.

"Yeah." He shoved his hands into his pockets. "Sometimes I wish —"

"That she were different?" Juli bit her tongue. *What a jerk. John picked someone to spill his heart out to and she came off like Superman.* "Sorry."

"It's okay." He watched more kids pile out of cars. "Don't ask me why I like Amy. Maybe because sometimes I get a look past the fluff and see loneliness."

Juli bit back the words "Fat chance" and wisely said nothing. Yet it did set her to wondering. Dad used to quote a Bible verse — 1 Samuel 16:7 — about people looking on the outside but God looking on the heart. John Foster was smart. If he felt that way about Amy, just maybe there was more to her than what everyone else saw.

"Joy to the world, the Lord is come!" Shannon sang out. The rest joined in. Juli knew she'd never forget the happiness in the faces of those they sang for. It gave her an idea. Back at the church for cocoa and cookies, she told the group, "It wasn't just the presents, but our presence, if you know what I mean. After the holidays, why don't we start our own Adopt-a-Grandparent program? You know, take them little gifts, but most of all, just go see them."

"Sounds great to me," Shannon quickly seconded the plan.

"Same here." "Me, too." "Imagine your

own grandkids not visiting you!" Before the evening ended, the youth group enthusiastically agreed to the idea.

When John and Ted dropped the girls off, this time at Shannon's, Ted laughed and commented, "Glad I'm not a UPS driver, having to deliver this late. Because of Christmas, I suppose. I'd rather go caroling." He grinned at Shannon.

Juli looked across the street, straight at a brown UPS van. Deliveries at ten o'clock at night? She tensed. The van sprang to life like a grizzly bear roused from hibernation and came straight toward the little group. Headlights pinned them with a glare, then swung away before the van made a U-turn and drove off.

Juli strained her eyes to see but the driver remained a dark shape with collar turned up and some kind of cap or hat over his or her eyes. She straightened. Her? What made her think the driver might be a woman?

"Come on, Juli." Shannon tugged at her arm. "I'm freezing."

Juli stumbled after her, holding back fear until they said good-night to Sean Riley and reached the haven of Shannon's room. "This sounds weird, but what if someone really is after me?"

"Why would they be?"

93

"I wish I knew. Maybe because of Dad." She hadn't realized how strong her subconscious had been considering this until it rushed out. The hollowness she'd felt when Dad died returned. "What if someone he arrested wants to get even? If only we knew what happened to him!"

"Maybe it's best if you never do," Shannon said soberly. "Anyway, whatever it was all about died with your father." Her eyes opened wider and darkened. "I'm the one with a banker for a father. Maybe the van's trailing *me,* not you."

Fresh horror spread through her. "Great. Now I can worry over kidnappers holding you for ransom, as well as seeing brown vans and gray men." Juli sagged.

The girls began to dress for bed.

"Juli, do you really, truly think you're in danger?"

Juli sighed. "It's more like scary clues warning that something bad is going to happen. I keep wondering if the nightmare is symbolic: the river eating away the ground beneath my feet, while the man just stands there waiting."

"You know dreams are always supposed to be the opposite," Shannon said. "We're leaving for Skagit House the day after tomorrow. No menace there!"

Except in my nightmare, Juli mentally added.

Two days later, Juli, Mom, Sean Riley, and Shannon climbed into Sean's roomy van. "We need the van to carry all our clothes and packages and stuff," Shannon said. "I wish we were there now!" She bounced on the seat next to Juli as her father turned the van south.

Juli silently echoed her wish, thinking of the miles that lay before them. She knew every part of the way as well as her own neighborhood. First came Mount Vernon, then east through several smaller towns. Finally, Rockport, where they took a secondary road south toward the mountain town of Darrington. There the road followed the wide, normally slow-moving Skagit River. Cottonwoods lined the rocky banks, broken here and there by sandbars just made for wiener roasts and beach parties. Around a sweeping curve of the river the Skagit House appeared, high enough on a rise to protect it from flood.

"I remember the first time I saw Skagit House," Juli said slowly. "I thought it looked like a smaller Tara from *Gone with the Wind.* It's still hard to believe an old-fashioned inn that offers gracious living and warm hospitality sits there in the least likely spot in the whole world."

Shannon giggled. "The first time I saw it I expected a butler to step out the carved front door. Or for Scarlett O'Hara to come sweeping down from the columned porch and onto the white-pebbled drive!"

"What's your favorite thing about Skagit House, Anne?" Sean Riley asked.

"Everything." Mom flung her arms wide. Her face looked more rested than since she'd gone back to teaching full-time, and her eyes sparkled with anticipation. "The southern-style meals where you can gain pounds just looking. The river. The fact that no shooting is allowed anywhere on the grounds except with a camera. I guess my very favorite thing is the wildlife. Deer that come to drink. Pheasant and grouse, robins, bluejays, and sparrows."

A rush of memories threatened to overwhelm Juli. Visits with Dad and Mom. Actually staying there with Shannon and her family. Watching the deer eat apples out of the housekeeper's hand and finally having a soft-eyed doe take shiny red fruit from her own palm. Now there would be new moments to treasure, some with Dave Gilmore. Juli felt warm color rise to her face.

A nudge from Shannon and the knowing

gleam in her eyes showed she suspected what Juli was thinking. "We're going to have a great time," she predicted. "Just wait and see."

"I know." Juli smiled back.

"It will certainly be peaceful with just family," Sean put in.

"Yes!" Shannon's arm shot into the air. "No homework. No strangers. Just two glorious weeks of winter sports and gathering around the fireplace." *And no brown UPS vans, gray men, or nightmares,* her understanding glance promised.

"Right," Juli agreed, vowing to forget her troubles and be happy. Not only for her own sake, but for Mom, who had valiantly carried on ever since Dad left on a snowy day much like this one — and never came home.

Chapter 8

Juli stretched and smiled when they swung into the curving driveway at Skagit House. The colonial mansion-style inn hadn't changed. Neither had the river. Water flow reduced by winter, it showed dark between snowy banks but didn't look treacherous. Neither had the Skagit gobbled up any of the property the way it had in Juli's nightmare.

A bubble of joy replaced the hard knot inside her. All this plus Dave Gilmore! What more could any girl in her right mind want? Besides, if she could find peace anywhere, it would be at Skagit House. Hadn't Shannon promised no homework, no strangers, freedom from fear?

Wrong. Ten minutes after the Rileys and Scotts arrived and gathered close to a roaring fire in the library, a scowling youngish man with brick-red hair strode past the open door.

"Come meet the family, Mr. Payne," Grand called. The man hesitated then marched into the comfortable room. Grand introduced each in turn.

Juli shot Shannon a glance, but her friend looked as bewildered as Juli felt.

Payne's piercing gaze swept over each of those gathered. "I'm sure everything will be fine." He marched out without any other greeting.

How rude! Juli instantly disliked the man, as much for his arrogance as the way he'd examined everyone present. *Like we were insects under a microscope,* she thought indignantly. Shannon's raised eyebrows and the way she rolled her eyes showed she felt the same way.

"Strange kind of lad," Grand told them. Wrinkles creased his forehead where a lock of snowy hair had fallen. "I said there'd be no fancies and he'd best go home. He said he had no family close by and would be for stayin'. I didn't have the heart to tell him he was nae welcome." Grand's "Riley blue eyes," as Juli secretly called them, twinkled. "Specially when he offered to pay double."

"Why would he do that?" Juli asked suspiciously. "Who is he, anyway?"

"Don't ask me," Shannon told her. "I haven't been here since Thanksgiving. What do you know about him, Grand?"

"Very little," Ryan Riley admitted. "His name's Andrew. He's nae one to mingle. He pays on time and takes care o' his own room. Says he wants no maids messin' about. His light burns late and at night I hear clickin' in his room."

"Could he be an author?" Juli wondered out loud.

"I canna say. He neither sends nor receives mail."

"He sounds mysterious," Shannon whispered to Juli when they grabbed their bags and headed up the fantastic curving staircase that led to the second floor. The northeast corner bedroom Shannon and Juli always shared had not one, but two canopied beds, its own bath and a walk-in closet big enough to hold clothes for an army. Juli cast an affectionate glance at the faded lavender brocaded walls and the pale green bedspreads and overhangs a master decorator had ordered to match. They even had tiny lavender flowers. The first thing she unpacked was Clue, who proudly sat at the head of the bed and surveyed the beautiful room.

Juli stopped unpacking long enough to run to the huge casement windows that offered a tremendous view of the back part of the property, which blended into forest. Birch and alder at the edge of the lawn gave way to fir, pine, cedar, and hemlock. Grand permitted no unnecessary cutting. "I'll nae be for takin' the wee folks' home," he always said, referring to the birds and squirrels, rabbits, and chipmunks that depended on the forest.

"Or the leprechauns'," Shannon usually reminded.

"Don't be makin' fun o' the little people," Grand told her. " 'Twas a pot o' gold when we found the Skagit House."

"See any leprechauns?" Shannon called to Juli from the closet.

"If there were such creatures, which there aren't, they'd be in Ireland."

"Mercy me! The wee folk follow an Irishman where e'er he goes." Shannon joined Juli at the window and gave a mock sigh. "No leprechauns."

"No animals, either." Juli reluctantly turned from the enchanting picture. "I'd better unpack. Grand left the tree for us to decorate, and we have to put our presents under it, and —"

"This is a vacation," Shannon protested. Mischief danced in her face. "Let's leave everything and go build a snowman. Race you. Last one downstairs is a rotten omelet." She ran from the window to the closet.

"Rotten *egg,* Shannon Riley." Juli groaned and dove for her ski suit. "When are you going to stop quoting, no, *mis*quoting those out-of-date clichés?"

Shannon had the last muffled word while pulling her parka over her head. "And deprive the world of Rileyisms? Never!"

They thundered down the stairs together and managed to squeeze through the front door at the same time. Jumping off the porch into the soft snow, they acted like five-year-olds until Juli saw something that abruptly ended her happiness. "Don't look, but we're being watched."

"Who? Where?" Shannon stood still but didn't turn.

"Andrew Payne," Juli hissed. "On the porch. Grab snow and chase me."

Shannon obeyed. Juli took off with Shannon at her heels, then swerved so abruptly toward the porch that Payne had no time to vanish. She halted on the top step. "Hello again, Mr. Payne," she panted. "Want to help build a snowman?"

Shannon's gasp was lost in Payne's grunt before he rudely brushed past them and marched down the steps.

"What's with him?" Shannon wanted to know, when he had moved out of hearing.

"I don't know." Juli stared until he disappeared around the side of the house.

Shannon looked anxious. "I hope having

one unpleasant person here doesn't spoil our vacation."

"We won't let it," Juli said fiercely. "If that brick-headed man thinks he's going to ruin everything, he can forget it." Anger and uneasiness gave way to an idea. "I know. Let's fix him up with Amy."

Shannon burst into laughter. "They deserve each other. Oh, no. Every time I see Mr. Payne I'll think of that and giggle."

"Just don't look at me or we'll disgrace ourselves," Juli warned. She glanced toward the side of the house. "I don't want to stay out any longer just now with him maybe watching from behind a tree."

"Let's get out of these snowy clothes and raid the fridge," Shannon suggested. "The cook promised to stock the pantry for us before she left. Grand said she acted like she thought we'd starve without her."

Juli gulped when they got to the old-fashioned kitchen and adjoining pantry. "It looks like a food bank!" A kettle of clam chowder that smelled heavenly simmered on the back burner of the enormous stove. A chocolate cake Ebenezer Scrooge would have given all his wealth to possess sat on the table. The freezer, fridge, and pantry shelves appeared to hold enough baked goods, meat, homemade pasta, fruit, and salad makings to fill a gymnasium.

Juli stared. "I've never seen this much food in one place at one time! Does your cook think we're in for a siege, like two or three months, maybe?" Why had she said that? A chill crept over her in spite of the well-lit, lovingly stocked pantry. Juli felt glad to join the others.

The dining room normally held a long refectory table. Now the six of them gathered around a small table set in the bay window against dark green drapes, drawn against the fading afternoon light. An arrangement of gold chrysanthemums tied with red ribbon sat in the center of the polished table.

"Mmm. Pretty. Where did they come from?" Juli asked.

"Didn't you bring them?" Grand looked puzzled.

Mom shook her head. "Not us. They look like they're from a florist."

A deep voice grated from Andrew Payne's side of the table. His gaze bored into Juli. "They came UPS."

Her fork clattered to the table. "UPS? How come a florist didn't bring them?" She shoved her shaking hands under the tablecloth and glared at him.

Payne shrugged. His steady gaze never left Juli's face.

"Who knows? Maybe the snow scared the delivery person. Maybe the driver's a friend of the florist." He casually added, "There are lots of UPS vans up here."

Shannon choked and reached for her glass of water. Juli stared straight back at Andrew Payne. *Don't worry about him,* a little voice whispered in her mind. *He may be nasty but it doesn't have anything to do with you.* But she didn't believe a word of it, or of Payne's bland explanations.

Except for Shannon, no one seemed to notice anything wrong. All except Andrew helped decorate the tree and hang woodsy-smelling cedar and pine swags with huge red bows. Later the girls curled up on their beds and Shannon told Juli, "There's probably a perfectly logical reason the flowers came UPS."

"Without a card? Aren't you a little suspicious that an anonymous bouquet gets delivered in a snowstorm by a UPS truck?"

"Maybe we should talk with Dad and Grand and Mom." Shannon's gray-blue eyes looked enormous above her turtleneck sweater of the same color.

Juli hugged her stretch pants-covered knees and scrunched further down in her soft white sweater. "Even if they believed me, what good would it do?"

"They could run out in the snowstorm shouting 'Who brought these flowers and where did they come from'?" Shannon weakly suggested.

Her desperate attempt to cheer Juli succeeded. "Can't you just see the headlines? 'IRATE PARENTS AND GRANDPARENT SURROUND BROWN VANS, DEMANDING PROOF THAT DRIVERS ARE REALLY UPS EMPLOYEES.' " The girls laughed hysterically until they cried.

When Skagit House grew quiet, Shannon and Juli sneaked their way down the staircase, lit only by a dim wall sconce that served as a night-light. Each carefully avoided looking at the other's packages, and it took several trips to get their gifts under the tree. By that time they were hungry again. "Any chopped apple cake and whipped cream left?" Juli wanted to know.

"Sure. Cheese and ham and rolls and pickles, too." Shannon put one hand over her mouth to keep from being heard. "The great food bandits strike again," she added when they'd made it back to their room with a well-laden tray. "No wonder we're hungry again. It's been the Dark Ages since dinner."

Juli choked on a crumb. "Not 'Dark Ages,' just ages."

"Whatever." Shannon grinned and

yawned. "I'll go ahead and shower while you finish. Christmas morning isn't all that far off."

"Okay." Juli slowly ate the rest of her cake, reveling in the spicy taste. When she finished she walked to the window and opened the drapes a crack to see if the snow had stopped falling.

Her heart leaped. Something had moved, close to the forest. A long, grotesque shadow, lengthened by the yard light, lay heavy on the white expanse of lawn between the woods and house. A second shadow stretched beside it.

Juli shoved a hand over her mouth to keep from shrieking. She raced noiselessly across the soft carpet to the light switch, flipped it, and ran back to the window. The shadows hadn't moved, but no matter how hard she tried, she couldn't see what made them.

Light streamed from the bathroom and Shannon came out. "What happened? Did a bulb burn out? Oh, you're enjoying the view."

"N— not really." Juli gave a last quick glance out the window. "It's pretty dark." Yet it hadn't been too dark for her to see how the second shadow faded and disappeared. The other changed into a man who strode with giant, arrogant footsteps toward the house. When he passed the yard light, Andrew Payne's grim face and set lips showed clearly in the yellow glow.

Should she tell Shannon? No, not yet. Shannon was already upset over having Andrew Payne around for the holidays. If she knew the brick-haired man was meeting someone outside in the snow, she'd be sure to tell her father and Grand. They'd ask Andrew to leave and Juli would never find out what was going on.

"I want to write mysteries," she whispered in Clue's ear after Shannon fell asleep. "Now's my chance to see how good I am at solving one. If only I were a super sleuth. Sounds cool, doesn't it? Juli Scott, Super Sleuth. Clue, what would a super sleuth do now?" She hugged her plushy friend and mumbled, "Like Scarlett O'Hara, I'll think about it tomorrow." She stifled a laugh. "Shannon would probably say 'day after tomorrow.' " She yawned again. "God, if there's really anything bad going on, would you please . . ."

She fell asleep before she could put into words what she wanted God to do.

The next morning's excitement made Juli forget the slightly sinister Andrew Payne's winter rendezvous. At least he'd been considerate enough not to barge in on the family's special gift opening time. He brusquely said he'd be there for Christmas dinner but spent the rest of the day off tramping through the woods. Juli battled the temptation to sneak into his third-floor room while he was gone but nobly restrained herself. A feeling she'd seen him sometime and somewhere teased at her brain. If only she could figure it out!

Grand and Sean had gone together to get the girls ski suits: red with black trim for Shannon; yellow with black for Juli. The Rileys had also added gift certificates for ski lessons and season passes for the tow chair at Mount Baker. Shannon gave Juli and Mom each a real Irish fisherman's knit sweater, then cried over her own gift. Mom and Juli had secretly spent hours making a special patchwork quilt. Backed with emerald green, it had the map of Ireland, complete with the river Shannon and a jaunty leprechaun.

"I'll keep it for my children and their children, as long as there's a Riley," Shannon choked out.

She turned holly berry red when Juli whispered, "They won't be Rileys. They'll be Smiths or Johnsons; maybe even Hiltons!"

Grand loved his wool muffler from the

Scotts. Sean had to dig for a tiny box hidden in layers of larger ones. It held a card: "Bearer is entitled to one home-cooked meal each month for the next twelve. Non-transferable."

"That's great!" He beamed at Mom.

He'd never looked at Mom like that before. Was he — did Mom — ? Why did she have to start worrying about that? Didn't she already have enough to handle? Resentment gnawed at Juli. She loved Shannon's father, but not for a dad. Her father wasn't dead. He couldn't be. When she got back to Bellingham, somehow she'd prove it. In the meantime, she didn't want Sean Riley or anyone else admiring her mother too much.

Everything got worse a few hours later.

Chapter 9

For some unexplainable reason, Juli wanted to be alone after dinner. She slipped outside into gray dusk and aimlessly scuffed through the snow between the inn and the sloping bluff that looked down on the Skagit River. She didn't think, just walked, knowing she couldn't stay out long. Darkness already shrouded the low hills behind Skagit House.

"Something's wrong," she whispered. "But what?" Below and to her left, the river murmured its way around the wide bend. She held her breath and turned right. A brown van stood half-hidden by a stand of pines.

Just like her dream. No. Then white birches had camouflaged the van. Juli rubbed her eyes and looked again. The birches were more to the right, naked and shivering in the wind. She looked back toward the pine thicket. A gray man stood watching her. Shabby gray coat. Gray hair. Gray face, as much as she could see in the shadows.

"What are you doing out here?" a harsh voice demanded.

Juli spun toward the sound, wondering if a person could actually die from fright. "I — I was just —"

"Better get inside," Andrew Payne ordered, eyes as unfriendly as his voice. "The dark's no place for a girl to be wandering around, especially in the snow."

"There's someone here who shouldn't be!" Juli told him furiously. "Right there by the pines." She jerked her thumb toward the thicket.

"I don't see anyone."

Juli whipped around. "Why . . ." Her voice faltered.

"Do you have hallucinations often?" Payne asked sarcastically.

"There was a man standing right there between me and the brown van." Juli's mouth dropped open. Even the growing darkness couldn't hide the fact that the pines concealed nothing. She turned back to Payne, catching a secretive smile. Then she heard the sound of grinding gears and the roar of a motor that quickly died. "You must at least have heard the van's motor," she triumphantly cried.

He cocked his head in a listening pose. "All I hear is the river."

In that moment, Juli hated Andrew Payne more than she had ever hated anyone in her entire life. Not just for lying, but because he was the only one who could confirm her story. She choked back a sob and fled to the house, up the stairs, straight to the bedroom she and Shannon shared. Luckily no one was in the hall or on the stairs.

"Juli, *what is it?*" Shannon gasped.

Juli laughed wildly. "The dream. The gray man. He said no one was there."

"The gray man? You talked with him?" Shannon's eyes widened.

"No. Andrew Payne. I know he saw the man and the van and heard the van drive away, but he lied." Frustration spilled like water from a faucet.

"I wonder why? Juli, what did the man do? Did he try to hurt you?"

"No. He just watched me. I was more scared of Andrew Payne than of him." Shock ran through her. "I really was!"

"We have to tell our folks. If someone's prowling, they need to know."

Juli shook her head violently. "Wait just a few days," she pleaded. "The other kids are coming tomorrow. We'll keep things so busy there won't be time for ghosts, although he can't be a ghost and drive a brown van." She giggled nervously. "What color is a ghost, anyway? Gray?"

"Probably more like bone-white."

"Thanks a lot. Just what I need to hear," Juli told her.

"Ask a dumb question and you get an unexpected answer," Shannon misquoted.

Juli didn't bother to correct her. If she were to get through the evening, she'd have to use all her drama skills and play a girl-who-loves-Christmas-and-being-with-family-and-friends role. She did so well that Shannon said later, "I wish I could hide my feelings the way you do. Everyone always knows how I feel." She laughed. "Now if you can do as well with Amy!" Juli just rolled her eyes.

How could a tall, blond boy get better looking in just a few days? she wondered when Dave's Mustang pulled in the next morning. Amy proudly rode in the bucket seat next to him, all smiles and smugness at having three boys to herself on the drive from Bellingham. John Foster and Ted uncurled their long legs from the cramped back seat and groaned.

"We'd have been here an hour sooner but Amy had trouble with her blow dryer and wouldn't come until it was fixed," Dave whispered in Juli's ear. She couldn't help grinning at the exasperation in his voice.

The boys unloaded the overstuffed trunk, mostly Amy's luggage. The tiny blond didn't offer to help. She'd discovered a new word: *"quaint."* The Skagit House was quaint. So were Grand, the snowman the girls had finally built, and the single room with the four-poster bed Shannon assigned to her.

"I could like her if she'd stop trying so hard," Shannon told Juli while the new arrivals unpacked.

"Really? What are you, a saint or something?"

"Why not? The Irish are really into saints." Shannon smiled wickedly. "I can see it now. St. Shannon's Day, celebrated right along with St. Patrick's Day."

She did an Irish jig and collapsed on her bed laughing.

Juli took time to throw a pillow at her before hunting for a headband. A brilliant sun had come out and she wouldn't want the hood of her new canary ski suit up all the time.

The hour before time to go in and help Mom with lunch flew past. An array of snow people stood on the front lawn, and a snow fight to end all snow fights left everyone starved. Even picky Amy ate as if it were her last meal, but had to wreck her good behavior by asking Grand, "Do we dress for dinner?"

His eyes twinkled. "Shure and you'll be for wearin' clothes for dinner, lunch, and breakfast. The Skagit House is a decent establishment. Besides, it's cold you'd be with out them!"

Everyone but Amy cracked up. She turned pink, pouted a little, then said, "You're so clever. Now I know why Shannon's like she is."

Whatever that's supposed to mean, Juli thought. "Hey, isn't it time to get the hat and draw for duty assignments?" she asked.

"Remember, I warned you all." Shannon gave a lilting laugh. "This is a vacation for Grand and Dad and Mom. If they want to help, fine. Otherwise we're on our own." She fixed a stern glance on the boys. "Can you cook?"

"Are you kidding?" Dave folded his arms across his chest. "I'm the best water-boiler in the Pacific Northwest."

"Good. Then you won't mind drawing for cooking as well as cleaning."

"Right." He reached into the hat and came up with a slip. "Yes! These are duties deluxe. I drew lunch tomorrow and there's a complete menu with directions."

"I took pity on everyone," Shannon admitted. "Actually, the cook left us so much food, cooking won't be hard. Also, the person doing meals can get others to help with peeling potatoes, setting the table, stuff like that. Mom and I are doing dinner tonight and we'll all help with dishes. These are tomorrow's jobs. Every day at lunch we'll draw different jobs. Even the best water-boiler in the Pacific Northwest doesn't get to cook all the time. No switching jobs, either."

Juli ended up with making beds. Amy drew last. "I have the smallest piece of paper." She made a face. "Clean bathrooms? I never clean bathrooms at home."

"Now you'll know how," Ted told her unsympathetically.

Juli wanted to cheer. A new and healthier relationship could form between the twins if Ted continued to stand up to Amy at least part of the time.

"Why aren't you drawing?" Amy pointedly asked Andrew Payne.

His reddish eyebrows shot up. "I pay my way and clean my own room." He shoved his chair back so sharply it sounded like an exclamation mark.

"Not very friendly, is he?" Amy said after he went out.

"He's a wet quilt and likes to be left

alone," Shannon explained.

"Don't you mean 'wet blanket'?" Mom asked when the shouts of laughter died.

"Who cares? Okay, people. Cleanup, then we hit the slopes."

To everyone's surprise, Amy said no more about cleaning the bathrooms. She just asked where the cleaning supplies were and what she was supposed to do.

"The staff cleaned everything before they left," Shannon told her. "When a girl gets bathrooms, she only has to clean yours, Mom's, Juli's and mine, plus the downstairs powder room. When a boy draws that job, he cleans Grand's, Dad's, the big one the boys are sharing, and the bath next to the kitchen."

"How did you work it?" Juli asked Shannon when they had a minute alone.

Shannon smirked. "I suspected Amy would go for the easiest job. The boys would naturally think it was on the smallest piece of paper and be polite. I wrote the bathroom assignment on the tiny slip. Just call me Sheer Luck Holmes."

For once, Juli didn't even bother to correct her. "I have to admit, Amy complained less than I expected." She considered for a moment. "Maybe my New Year's resolution should be to try and like her, not just tolerate her because she's in our youth group. You know, love your enemies and all that."

"Good idea. If she responds, it means a better vacation." Shannon grinned like a pixie. "If not, your being nice to her will drive her crazy!"

The next day flashed past at jet-speed. No brown vans or lurking strangers haunted Skagit House. Juli breathed a sigh of relief. Maybe whatever had been happening was over. She hoped so. Constantly looking over her shoulder and being afraid trouble might come any moment was *not* fun.

"This may interest you, Juli," Mom said a few days after Christmas. "It's an article on the value of keeping a journal. I'm considering trying it. I like what the author advises. 'Don't write diary-like, today-I-did-this stuff. Go off by yourself where it's quiet. Record important happenings. Especially write your feelings, both good and bad. Write when you feel the need to write, not just because you feel you should. Unless you choose to share your journal, no one will ever see it but you and God, so be totally honest. Putting things on paper helps you feel free.' "

"I might try it, too," Juli said.

"I just happen to have an extra notebook and pen," Mom teased. A sheepish smile crossed her face. "I bought them when I got a set for myself."

That night after Shannon had fallen asleep, an urgency to begin her journal filled Juli. She quietly slipped downstairs, carrying the brand new notebook and pen. Dying embers in the library fireplace welcomed her. Juli turned on a reading lamp, wrapped herself in an afghan, and curled into the corner of the couch. For a long time she stared into the red coals. When she finally picked up her pen and began to write, words raced across the first page.

I saw the gray man outside my window tonight. He comes and goes, melting into the rising river fog until he's just a curious trick of mist, especially when I call Shannon to the window. If only he were a shadow, or a ghost, or anything except gray! If only Shannon could see him, just once. We still haven't told our families. She says she believes me but I can't help wondering. Does she think way down deep that I'm imagining him? Or is she remembering what I told her about blacking out after Dad died?

Sometimes. I'm not even sure of myself. Maybe I'm going crazy. Everyone says you're always the last to know. God, are You here? Do You believe me?

If he'd only do something! Break into the house or try to attack me. I could scream and hang onto him. People would rush to help and see for themselves. How can they protect me against something that may not exist?

The gray man never comes any closer to the house than the fringe of trees across the backyard. He appears at dusk, usually, and blends into the twilight. It's almost as though he knows when I'll be alone and watches for me. Then he watches ME. Even when I pull the drapes or shades, I can still feel shadowy eyes that must be gray, watching and watching and watching.

I'm writing this all down so if anything happens to me the police will be sure to question Andrew Payne. He continues to eat with us, but we — including Grand — don't know anything more about him than we did when he first came. It's almost worse having him watch me than the gray man. He does, too, every time he thinks I'm not looking. Sometimes when I glance up and see his gaze boring into me, I think I'll scream.

Earlier today I saw Andrew Payne stalking across the yard. I followed. He spoke to someone. All I heard was the end. ". . . you fool!" The underbrush rustled and he came charging out and shouted, "Are you spying

*on me?" I didn't answer. I just wish I could
remember where I've seen him . . .*

Juli slowly closed the notebook. The fire had
long since died. The growing chill of the
room thrust through the afghan. She laid the
afghan aside, turned off the light, and started
up the stairs with her precious journal. A
board creaked behind her. She froze. Silence
followed. She took another step. A board
creaked again.

"It's probably Andrew Payne, snooping
around," Juli whispered. "Well, I won't give
him the satisfaction of knowing I heard
him." She tiptoed on upstairs, down the
hall, and to her room. She opened and
closed the door, but instead of going inside,
she flattened herself against the wall and
prayed not to be seen.

A few moments later, a man's figure appeared at the top of the stairs. Andrew
Payne didn't look right or left, but made the
turn and started up to the third floor. His
wet coat glistened in the dim hall light.

When he had gone, Juli went inside the
bedroom and groped her way to the bed.
She laid her notebook on the bedside stand,
grabbed Clue, and burrowed under the
covers, glad for the warmth. *You have to tell
Mom and the Rileys,* her conscience prodded.

Tell them what? a second voice scornfully countered. *That you're seeing ghosts, and the star guest at Skagit House is up to something weird?* She fell asleep with the voices still arguing.

A gentle shake roused her. A laughing voice was saying, "Morning has broken and it's beautiful. Wake up, Cinderella."

"Sleeping Beauty, not Cinderella," Juli mumbled. She stretched. Memory of the night before stiffened her body. Her eyes popped open. She raised up in bed and reached for her journal.

It was gone.

Chapter 10

Juli stared at the empty spot where she had laid her journal the night before. Shock gave way to rage. How dare Andrew Payne creep in while she and Shannon slept and steal her journal, her secret thoughts! Ice formed in her blood. What would he do, now that he knew she suspected him?

Shannon stopped brushing her hair. "You're awfully quiet this morning."

Juli started to blurt out her loss. She bit her lip. Shannon might give in about not reporting a mysterious gray man, but she wouldn't stand for Juli being ripped off by a red-headed jerk. "Uh, you didn't see a notebook, did you?"

"This one?" Shannon picked it up off the floor. "How come it's under your bed?"

Relief flooded through Juli. "It must have fallen off the stand. Thanks." She hesitated. "I — it's my journal. Mom said I might want to start one."

"Great," Shannon agreed. "Next time you need an idea for Mrs. Sorensen's class, you'll have it all written down." She tossed her brush aside. "Get moving, okay? No breakfast in bed at Skagit House!"

Juli quickly showered, threw on jeans and a sapphire Hillcrest Pirates sweatshirt, and did her hair. The eyes that stared back from the mirror reflected the color of the sweatshirt and looked bluer than ever. "Just for today I'm going to take a holiday from mystery," she told Clue. "Hey, neat title. Wonder if Mrs. Sorenson will like it?" A dozen ideas for a story, "Mystery Takes a Holiday," swam through her head.

Juli glanced around the room, looking for a good hiding place to put her journal. Shannon would never read it in a million years. Juli couldn't be as sure about Amy, if she drew bed-making. She finally hit on just the right place. No one would look for buried treasure in a canvas tote bag beneath a pile of clean socks. Juli smiled and ran downstairs, humming as she went.

After breakfast and chores, the laughing group headed outside again for a day of fun. Following dinner, they decided to make a triple batch of fudge. Amy watched. Shannon and Juli measured. "I'll wash the pan," Dave volunteered.

"Only because you get the leavings," Shannon told him. She handed it over in spite of loud howls of protest from the others. "Here, Ted, set the candy outside. It will be cool in a few minutes."

A good share vanished at the still-warm stage. Dave reached for yet another piece and grinned at Juli. "Let's go for a moonlight walk. You'll be a balloon if you don't get some exercise."

"It wasn't *me* who ate six pieces of fudge," Juli protested.

"It wasn't I," Dave corrected.

"Right. *You* ate a dozen, maybe more!" Lighthearted and happy, Juli asked, "Who else wants to go out into the cruel, cold world?" She changed her voice to that of a race track announcer. "Ladies and gentlemen, Ted Hilton is already racing for the stairs, with Shannon close behind. He's halfway up; no, he's at the top. So is she. There they go down the hall, feet pounding like —"

Amy shivered and moved closer to the fire. "Why don't we just stay in and watch TV? It's so cold. Look at the icicles hanging in the windows."

"You can watch TV at home," Ted told her from the doorway.

Juli saw the look in John's face and decided to help him out. "John, did I hear you coughing earlier? Maybe you should stay in."

"Maybe I should. I don't want to miss all the skiing and stuff tomorrow." He dropped down to the rug by Amy's chair and sent Juli a grateful glance.

"Forsooth, you are deceitful," Dave told Juli when the door closed behind the brave foursome. "See how well I'm doing with my Shakespeare?"

Juli giggled. "Shouldn't it be 'Forsooth, thou art deceitful'? Besides, I didn't say John coughed. I only asked if he did."

Dave just laughed. "Sure is a great place, isn't it?"

"Yeah." Juli looked at the high-flying moon above the dark branches heavy with snow, the stars trying to outshine the moon, the almost-silent Skagit swishing past below. A sting in the air tickled her nose, and the walkers' feet crunched on the hard-crusted snow. Shannon and Ted plowed along behind, then paused to argue over what game they should play after the walk.

Juli took in a deep breath of contentment. *What a perfect night!* She stiffened. *Oh, no. Had something moved in the shadows?*

"Juli, what's wrong?" Dave stopped dead still. "You're off in another world. What's up?"

Could she tell him? Well, maybe a part of it. "Something weird is going on."

Dave lowered his voice and bent over so the others wouldn't hear. "I think so, too. I woke up in the night, thirsty enough to drink the river dry. I didn't want to run water in our bathroom and wake John and Ted, so I sneaked downstairs. I thought I heard voices on the long porch Amy calls a verandah.

"I unlocked the front door and stepped out. There was no one there, but a vehicle without lights was coasting down the driveway. A motor started." He scuffed his boots in the snow. "I'd have said something, only I saw Andrew Payne slipping around back and figured it must be okay. I came inside, waited until he went upstairs, and sneaked back to bed. Should I tell the Rileys?"

"I guess not." Juli knew she didn't sound very convincing.

"If you need help solving a mystery, I'm your man," Dave bragged. "I aced my Junior Detective kit when I was nine."

"Thanks," she mumbled.

"So where and when do we start?"

"Probably just by watching and acting like there isn't anything wrong."

"I'll need to hang around you a lot, so we can plan our strategy," Dave said. "Any objections? Private investigators have to stick together."

Juli's pulse beat faster. "No objections. It's a good idea." *More like marvelous, fantastic, terrific,* she silently added.

"Okay." He dropped a long arm around her shoulders and gave her a quick hug. "Scott and Gilmore, P.I.s. As soon as we clear up our first case, we'll sell miniseries rights to NBC and get famous." He dropped his arm and called to Ted and Shannon, "We'd better go in. Juli's shivering."

She caught Shannon's grin, but her friend didn't mention it until they were curled up on their twin beds after games and more fudge. Then she innocently asked, "Isn't it funny how a warm hug gives a girl the cold shivers?"

"You saw?" Juli felt her smile widen.

"Yes!" Shannon gave a victory signal. "If you'll lend me your black sweatshirt tomorrow, I'll tell you something."

"Sounds like blackmail to me," Juli couldn't help answering.

Shannon rolled her eyes. "Cute. Do you want to hear, or don't you?" When Juli nodded, she said, "I found out why Dave's the way he is. About you, I mean. Ted said Dave's liked you since junior high but figured he didn't have a chance because you're so popular."

Juli's mouth fell open. "No way!"

Shannon looked wise. "Boys talk, too, you know."

Juli fell back on her pillow and stared at the canopy. "This is incredible! I thought he just hugged me because —" She nearly blurted out too much.

"Because he hugs every girl he knows? Don't be dumb. Dave Gilmore's not like that." Shannon's lilting laughter rang out. She stifled it in her pillow. When she came up for air, her whole face sparkled with mischief. "Amy's sure given him plenty of chances." She laughed again. "May the best man come in first."

"You mean 'May the best man win,' only in this case, it's the best girl," Juli told her. "Thanks, I will!" She grabbed Clue and hugged him. "You really made my day, but what about you and Ted?" She looked at her friend, privately wondering how any boy could keep from being crazy about her. She looked positively beautiful in an apricot-colored sleep shirt.

Shannon turned serious and hugged her knees. "I'm pretty sure he likes me. A lot. Someday when it's the right time, I hope to marry the kind of man I think Ted will become. He's a real Christian. So is Dave."

"I know what you mean." Juli sat up again. Now that they were growing up, would it mean a change in their friendship? For one wild moment Juli wanted to stop the clock. Right then. She couldn't bear to think the future might separate her from Shannon. The thought went through her like the dark, hidden currents beneath the Skagit. "Shannon, will you promise me something?"

She looked surprised. "Of course."

Juli realized the difference between them. If Shannon had asked, she'd have wanted to know what before promising. "No matter what happens, let's not ever let anything make our friendship mean less than it does right now."

"We won't. We'll be like two women I knew in Ireland. Erin and Katie were friends, just like we are. They went to school and roomed together at college. They also dreamed of one day living next to each other and raising their children to be friends. Yet they knew such dreams seldom come true." Sadness shadowed her eyes.

"Did theirs?" Juli hugged Clue tighter and held her breath.

"Yes. Both girls married. They separated for a time, but their husbands came to know and like each other. Years later, Erin, Katie, and their families built houses side by side. Those homes still stand." Shannon blinked long lashes. "When my mother Katie died, it was Erin who comforted me most."

Juli swallowed hard.

"If life is for bein' good to us, we'll do the same." Shannon didn't notice she'd fallen into Irish brogue.

"Even if miles should come between us, we'll be together," Shannon vowed.

Juli fell asleep to the memory of Shannon's promise and Dave's unexpected offer of help mingling with the creak of Skagit House as it settled for the night. No shadowy gray figures or unfriendly brick-haired men haunted her dreams. How could they, when people who cared for Juli surrounded her? And when the prayer of thankfulness she whispered brought a blanket of peace?

Juli's favorite story opening in the whole world was from Charles Dickens' *A Tale of Two Cities*, an outside reading assignment the year before. The Skagit House party fit the beginning perfectly: "It was the best of times, it was the worst of times." For every best came a worst, dark blotches to tarnish the shine of the holidays. Ping-Pong and charades. Skiing. Bonfires and skating, after the snow stopped and a hard freeze made the pond behind Skagit House safe.

"I read an article where an old-timer said

the Sauk River near Darrington, which is less than twenty miles up the road, froze so solid he drove a team and wagon across," John said. "It must have been some winter!"

"The Skagit River never freezes that deeply," Grand said. "Stick to the pond."

Juli noticed how often her mother skated with Sean Riley. Mom looked more like her sister, with her cold-reddened cheeks and eyes all sparkly from the exercise. Sometimes it depressed Juli. Was Mom forgetting Dad? She began observing carefully, searching for clues that Mom cared too much for Shannon's father. To her great relief, Mom acted no different with Sean than when she skated with one of the tall basketball players.

A big disappointment was that so far Scott and Gilmore, P.I.s, had discovered little, although Juli had told Dave about the gray man. Dave still hadn't seen the intruder but assured Juli he believed she really had seen him. "The only thing I've learned from spying nights is that the UPS van isn't what it seems," he said one morning when he and Juli had a private moment in the kitchen. "Last night I got close to the van by dodging from tree to tree. The logo has been painted over! People don't paint out logos just for fun, Juli. It's time to tell the Rileys and your mom."

"Wrong," said a voice behind them. *"Keep your snooping to yourselves!"*

Juli turned so fast she backed into Dave. Andrew Payne stood just a few feet away, jogging shoes damp and noiseless on the tiled kitchen floor.

"Who are you to tell us what to do?" Dave's eyes flashed fire. "You've been sneaking around ever since you came here."

"If you don't keep your mouth shut, you'll bring tragedy to a lot of people."

Payne took one step backward. Another. He backed out the door, still glaring. His threat hung heavy in the formerly secure kitchen.

"That's it. We're reporting." Dave started toward the living room.

Juli grabbed his arm. "No! We need to talk about what he said. He sounded like he knew what he was saying." She tried to think. "I don't know why, but somehow I get the feeling he might not be a crook after all."

"I don't think so, either, even though I don't like the guy." Dave slammed one fist into his other hand. "If I could just catch that gray man of yours!"

Just then Ted and Shannon burst into the kitchen, John and Amy right behind. "Grand is taking us for an old-fashioned sleigh ride!" Shannon caroled. "Would you believe he's arranged for horses and a sleigh big enough for all of us?"

Late that afternoon, the entire house party bundled up for the sleigh ride. Amy tried her best to sit by Dave but he outmaneuvered her by dropping down between Juli and Shannon. John, who had quietly watched the whole scene, loosed a thunderbolt by announcing, "I'm going to help Grand drive the team."

She turned a startled face toward him. "You mean I won't have a date?"

"We're all just going as a group," Shannon put in.

Amy played her high card. "I'm not. I'll stay home."

"Fine. You can keep Andrew Payne company. If he's here, that is. I haven't seen him since we ate lunch." John climbed up by Grand, leaving her staring.

"I'll have to go along; I can't stay here alone." These were the last words Amy, the self-imposed martyr, spoke on the entire ride.

Juli refused to worry about her. Jagged ridges slashed the winter sky. The jingle of sleigh bells blended with laughter and singing. It gave her a feeling of good will, in spite of Amy's pouting. Juli felt totally secure, with Dave on one side of her and Sean Riley on the other. At last John, who had proven to be a good sleigh driver, clucked to the horses and turned them toward home. They arrived just before dusk. John stopped with a flourish in front of the Skagit House. "All out."

"What on earth!" Grand leaped down from the sleigh and ran toward the inn. The alarm in his voice sent an icy chill down Juli's back. "What is it?" She climbed out and stared at the Skagit House. The carved door Grand had carefully locked before leaving stood wide open!

"Stay back," Sean warned. He jumped from the sleigh and followed Ryan Riley into the dark, menacing hall beyond the yawning, telltale front door.

Chapter 11

"What are we doing out here when they may need help?" Dave yelled. He took off up the walk to the porch, with John just a few steps behind.

Amy clutched Ted's arm when he started after them. "You can't leave us alone," she wailed. "You don't know who might be in there."

He jerked free. "Whoever's in there isn't out here." Ted followed the others.

Amy promptly burst into tears. She looked so small and frightened, Mom took pity on her. "We'll be all right, Amy." She handed Amy a tissue. The blond cheerleader's sobs faded to sniffles during what Juli felt must be the longest five minutes of their lives. Juli hoped she didn't look as ghastly as she felt. Yet a sense of relief filled her. Now everyone would know something was terribly wrong at Skagit House, without her or Dave saying a word.

"Come in, but don't touch anything," Grand called from the porch.

Juli followed the others on reluctant feet. Inside the hall, she stopped and stared. In the short time they'd been gone, someone or something had turned the inn into a disaster area. Half-melted snow puddles spread on the polished hall floor. Books by the score had been torn from shelves and cluttered the library floor. Many had crumpled pages. Pictures hung crooked on the walls.

Not a downstairs room had been spared. In the kitchen, the electric burners had been removed and tossed aside. Upstairs was no better. Bathroom cabinets hung open. Pillows minus cases had been flung about. Mattresses tilted at crazy angles. Clue rested on one ear, his perky red plaid ribbon untied.

Juli waited until the others moved on from Shannon's bedroom before she flew to her tote bag. In spite of Grand's warning, she reached under the pile of socks that gaped from its open mouth. Her notebook lay closed and apparently undisturbed. "Why?" Juli whispered. "Did we scare him off when we came home?" A nervous chill went through her. She hastily replaced the socks and ran after the others, unwilling to be alone.

When Juli got downstairs, Sean Riley was talking into the phone. "As far as we can determine, nothing was taken. No, it doesn't look like the work of kids. It's a complete mystery. Why would anyone search Skagit House?" Sean's strained face little resembled the carefree man who'd sung loudly with the rest.

More of Juli's "worst of times" came when the police arrived. They swarmed like bees in a wildflower patch, fingerprinting everyone and dusting for prints. When Juli timidly asked, "Are you finding anything?" the officer with eyes like shiny steel drills just grunted. Juli wished she'd kept quiet.

Dave beckoned her to the porch, away from the others. "Is it our fault?"

"What could we have told them? About a gray man no one else sees? A UPS van that isn't a UPS van? Or that we suspect Andrew Payne —"

"Looking for me?" the stocky man asked from the bottom step.

Juli choked back a scream. He'd come from nowhere, and *who was with him?*

"Meet my sister Mary," Andrew said. "She just flew in from Seattle. I knew she'd be welcome here." His unsmiling mouth dared anyone to disagree.

To avoid answering, Juli turned to Mary. Brownish hair. Average face. Ordinary figure. Only the sharpness of her gaze resembled Andrew's. Juli felt scorched by it before Mary said, "If Andy hadn't told me of the famous Riley hospitality, I'd have felt I was intruding, what with it being the holidays."

Juli mumbled something and Andrew swept Mary past them and into the inn. He couldn't be guilty of tearing the place up. He'd brought his alibi. But wait. Wasn't Mary's arrival just a little too convenient?

Dave reacted violently. He grabbed Juli's hand, led her inside, and told her, "That's it. We're settling this right now, while the police are here."

The officers courteously listened, but even Juli realized how pitifully little she and Dave knew. When put into words, their suspicions and flimsy facts added up to a heap of nothing. Juli saw disbelief on the officers' faces and cried, "If nothing is going on, why did Andrew Payne warn us not to say anything?" She saw a strange look pass between Andrew and the officer in charge, but couldn't interpret it.

Andrew looked at Mary and the first real laugh Juli ever heard from him rolled out. His eyes twinkled, "I couldn't resist. Here they were making a mystery out of shadows. A warning couldn't help adding to the excitement."

Either he doesn't know or he's the world's most convincing liar, Juli thought sourly. Juli hated to admit it but truth rang in every word. He couldn't have known.

"Andy's a great one for jokes," Mary explained.

"It's nae funny," Grand said sternly.

Payne looked down but not before Juli saw a glint in his eyes that certainly wasn't repentance.

"Maybe he's a Dr. Jekyll that runs and hides," Shannon whispered.

Too churned up inside to correct her, Juli burst out, "I wish he *would* run and hide, anywhere except at Skagit House! He must know no one wanted him for the holidays. Now he's brought his sister."

"If she really is," Juli told Dave later. "There's no way of finding out. The airline wouldn't tell us if they had a Mary Payne on their passenger list."

"The police officer in charge said something real low to Payne. Andrew nodded, then said, barely loud enough for me to hear, 'My room wasn't touched. Probably because I always lock my door.' The officer didn't answer. The Rileys said there's never been any trouble here before. That's part of what makes Skagit House so popular. So how come Andrew Payne locks his door?"

"I'd give a bundle to find out," Juli muttered. The beginning of an idea came. "What's the penalty for breaking and entering?"

"Stiff." Dave's mouth curved in a conspiratorial smile. "On the other hand, if someone just happened to go in to clean . . ." He grinned even more.

"How? He cleans his own room." Yet the idea gripped Juli with eagle claws and hung on, all through the rest of the police investigation.

"Better cut the vacation short and send these people back home," the officer in charge advised. "There has to be more behind this than we can determine at this point. Someone wants something mighty bad to break in here at the exact time everyone's gone and do such an extensive search."

"We can't leave any too soon for me," Amy said shrilly. "Let's pack and go."

"Not tonight," Sean Riley told the guests. "It's too late. Father and I'll stand guard and we'll leave in the morning."

"I'm not sleeping alone in a room that's been vandalized," Amy flatly stated.

"Mary can use the second bed in your room," Andrew Payne suggested.

"I guess that's okay." Amy shot a sidewise

glance toward Shannon and Juli, obviously hoping to be invited to stay with them. Neither said anything. Twin beds and three girls meant one on the floor, and Juli could just bet who that person wouldn't be!

"How does Payne know how many beds there are in Amy's room?" Dave hissed in Juli's ear when the police went out and the others headed upstairs to strip the beds and remake them.

"You tell me." Juli managed a sickly grin. "Things just keep getting 'curiouser and curiouser,' as Alice in Wonderland said, don't they? I wish we didn't have to leave tomorrow. It doesn't give time for Scott and Gilmore, P.I.s, to investigate. I wonder if Grand would let at least some of us stay?" She hopefully added, "The staff's still on vacation and this place needs mega cleanup."

To her complete astonishment, Andrew Payne suggested much the same thing the following morning at breakfast. Wonder of wonders, he and Mary joined in to help prepare the meal. At the table he said, "Mr. Riley, no one in their right mind would show up here again after tearing the place apart. And you need help cleaning up. Mary and I'll be glad to pitch in, and some of the others might, too.'"

"Not me!" Amy's fork clattered to her

plate. Her light blue eyes darkened with determination. "I'm getting out of here as fast as Dave can drive me."

"Sorry, Amy. If the Rileys agree, I'd like to stay." Dave reached for his juice.

"Same here," Ted quickly added.

"Who's going to take me home?" she demanded. "I won't stay here where creeps can walk right in and go through my stuff!"

John Foster looked troubled. Juli suspected he was torn between wanting to remain at Skagit House and pleasing Amy. "If it's all right with Dave, I can take you home in the Mustang," he told her.

Andrew Payne looked so pleased, Juli immediately grew suspicious. What was he, some kind of puppeteer, dangling them all on strings of his making? Why did Andrew suddenly seem so anxious for them to stay, when until now he acted like nothing in the world would please him better than to get rid of them? Instantly the look vanished, and Payne casually said, "Mary needs to run in to Bellingham. She can take anyone who decides to go. That way, you won't be short one car when the holidays are over."

What an out, thought Juli, furious. Maybe Andrew and "sister Mary" had actually trashed the inn, then just pretended to arrive after the others returned. Well, she wasn't getting away with it. "Would it be all right if I went with you?" she asked, amazed at how normal her voice sounded. "I can stop by the house, get the mail, and pick up some more games." It sounded lame even to her. If only Dave or Shannon would catch on and help her out.

To her relief, Dave immediately said, "Mail. Ha! I've beaten you at every game here so you're running home to get others." He laughed. "Bring on your new games, Juli, but it won't do any good. I'll win those, too."

"Excuse me," Amy's cold voice cut in. "I have to pack." Without offering to help clean the table, she slid from her chair and stalked up the stairs.

"Shannon and Ted and I'll do your chores," Dave volunteered. "Go get ready." Understanding shone in his eyes and something else that made Juli feel special. She started from the dining room, wondering what on earth she could talk about with Mary on the long ride back to Skagit House from Bellingham.

"I'll be right back." Shannon followed Juli into the hall. "Are you up to something?" she whispered.

"Watch Andrew Payne. If you get a chance, sneak into his room."

"What am I supposed to find?" Shannon looked puzzled.

"I don't know. Anything suspicious." Juli saw Mary coming toward them and raised her voice. "We shouldn't be gone all that long. Grand said he heard a weather report and the roads are clear."

Amy, parked in the front passenger's seat, of course, chattered over her shoulder to John all the way to Bellingham.

Probably trying to make up for ignoring him all week, Juli guessed. Sympathy caused Juli to ask, "Are you going back with us, John? You're welcome, you know."

"Thanks, I —"

Amy's honey-smooth voice interrupted. "We should probably use the extra time to work on ideas for the youth group's Valentine banquet," she said. "Once school and activities start again, we won't have a lot of extra time."

John grinned at Juli. "Amy's right. Guess I'll stay."

Juli saw Mary Payne's mouth twitch. Somehow it made her seem more human. She drove competently, as Juli suspected she did everything else. Was she really Andrew's sister? Why not? Even unfriendly people had family. Juli sat bolt upright.

Hadn't Grand said he felt sorry for Payne? That he let Andrew stay at the inn even when it was closed because "the lad" had no family? One way or the other, Andrew Payne had lied.

A lifetime later, Mary dropped Amy and John off, then drove to Juli's. The troubled girl crawled out of the station wagon in front of her house and relaxed. With all that had happened, she wouldn't have been surprised to find their home had also been ransacked.

"I'll do what I need to, and pick you up in about an hour," Mary quietly said.

Strange. Mary's business had been important enough to make a trip clear from Skagit House, yet she could handle it in less than an hour. Juli longed to stick with her like Krazy Glue, but couldn't think of a way to pull it off. All she could do was say, "Okay, and thanks," then watch the wagon until it turned a corner.

Juli slowly walked to the porch, relieved to see no footprints in the snow covering the front yard. Inside, she shivered and turned up the thermostat in her bedroom. No sense heating the whole house. She wouldn't be there that long. The mail accumulated beneath the mail slot consisted of just Christmas cards and some bills, but provided an alibi for coming.

Now for the games. Juli headed for the den. Why she opened the blinds rather than switching on the lights, she never knew. The second she did, a blur outside the window sent her heart to her throat. Forgetting caution, she ran from the den to the kitchen, unlocked the door, and stepped outside. "Who are you and what do you want?" she yelled. It came out as a whisper and floated away on the empty air, the same way the gray man always disappeared. But not quite. This time she saw tracks — and something else. A soiled scrap of paper lay at her feet, barely visible against the snow.

Juli snatched it up, hurried back inside, and relocked the door before reading the scrawled words that burned into her brain:

Meet me at the usual place. Bring it. You know what happens if you don't.

Juli turned over the torn and wrinkled paper. Her knees felt weak and it was hard to breathe. She dropped to a kitchen chair, shocked not by the bold writing but by the penciled message on the back: *This is the last time!!!*

Her father's writing. Even more condemning, the use of three exclamation marks. Juli had told Dad over and over only one punctuation mark goes at the end of a sentence, but he always stressed important things by using three. Each got bolder and darker, until the last almost drove through the page.

What did it mean? Why had Dad written such a message? *And when?* How had it. ended up in the backyard? The gray man? Of course! He must have dropped it.

The doorbell echoed through the house and set her already-strained nerves on edge. "Coming!" Juli stuffed the paper inside her sweater, cringing when it touched her skin, and ran to the front door. "I've got to turn down the heat in my bedroom," she told Mary. "I'll be out in a minute." Was that a shade of disappointment on the other's face before she turned back?

"Please, God, help me act natural," Juli prayed. She quickly closed the blinds in the den and lowered her bedroom thermostat. Next she tossed the mail and a half-dozen games into a large tote bag and reset the alarm system. Finally, Juli went back to the station wagon and the doubtful security of Mary Payne. Only God could keep her from betraying her fear during the long ride to the inn.

Chapter 12

To Juli's surprise, Mary turned out to be a good traveling companion. She asked questions about school, commented on what a wonderful place Skagit House was, and said how glad she felt to be there. "It's such a relief to get away from everything," she confessed.

"Even though you ran into a crime scene?" Juli asked point-blank. She held her breath waiting for the answer.

Mary laughed. "I have to admit any hint of a mystery always intrigues me."

"Really? Me too." Juli found herself relaxing. After that, the conversation flowed smoothly.

When they reached the small town of Rockport, Mary pulled off the road and parked in front of a convenience store. "We'll gas up here."

Juli wondered why she hadn't filled the tank before they left Bellingham, but politely said nothing except, "After last night's excitement, I'm so sleepy I can hardly keep my eyes open." She yawned.

"Take a nap, if you like." Mary reached under the seat for her purse.

"Maybe I will." Juli leaned her head back and closed her eyes. A muffled thud followed by a clinking sound brought them open again. "What's that?"

"Sorry. I dropped my purse." Mary bent to scoop up the spilled contents.

Why should dropping a purse bring a strained note to Mary's voice? Juli glanced at her. Was that — yes! She was stuffing tissues and lipstick and coins back in next to a *gun!* Why would anyone carry a weapon on a visit to see her brother? Juli's suspicion grew more acute. Andrew Payne wasn't Mary's brother, although she obviously was mixed up in his secret doings.

She bit her lip to keep from demanding, "What are you doing with a gun in your purse?" Common sense warned her she must not let on that she'd seen it. Juli quickly closed her eyes. "Wonder what's happening at Skagit House?"

She heard the relief in Mary's voice when she replied, "Major cleanup." Her laugh sounded forced. "We missed some of it."

"Yeah." Juli deliberately yawned again. "We'll be there soon. Glad the weather held for us." That should be trite enough to calm any suspicions Mary might have. It did nothing to lessen the icy chill stealing into Juli. People carried guns for two reasons: self-defense, or because they planned to use them.

"What should I do, God?" she prayed. Her whisper sounded loud in the empty car. "She hasn't threatened me. A lot of women carry guns now, especially those who live in large cities. Besides, if Mary really is dangerous and I ask for help from the store clerks, she might do something to them." If only Dave were with her. Or Shannon, whose practical advice helped still unfounded suspicions. Juli hid her trembling hands in the pockets of her jacket and pretended to sleep. She heard Mary slide in behind the wheel. The station wagon pulled back onto the road. Juli's nerves screamed until the wagon made the correct turn. Then she sat frozen, ready to yank open the door and fling herself out, if Mary slowed or stopped along the now-deserted stretch of highway leading to Skagit House.

While Juli fought fear with prayer, Shannon had troubles of her own. The command Juli gave before she left rested on her friend's shoulders like a boulder. "Thinking about solving mysteries is fun," Shannon told herself, stuffing a pillow into its case and throwing it back on her bed. "Sneaking into Andrew Payne's room to snoop isn't! Even telling myself how much Juli needs me doesn't make it easier. I don't have a clue about being a spy." She grabbed Juli's stuffed bear and giggled nervously. "Excuse me, Clue! Do you have any ideas?"

"Talking to yourself?" Dave teased from the doorway.

Shannon felt herself redden. "Yeah. I mean, Juli asked me to do something for her and I don't know how."

Dave came inside and lowered his voice. "Something about Andrew Payne?"

Shannon cheered up. "How did you know?"

"I know some of his excuses are so lame it's almost funny," Dave told her. His usually laughing blue eyes remained serious. "Shannon, we've got to find out who he is and what he's doing here. The same for his so-called sister. I know some of what Juli says sounds wild, but there are things going on. She's not crazy, and she's not imagining things."

"I'm so glad you believe her!" Shannon cried. She felt hope surge through her. "If we could only prove Andrew isn't who he says he is." She made a face. "Although he hasn't ever come right out and said much about himself."

"That's even more suspicious," Dave said. "He has to be hiding something."

Shannon looked at the open door and dropped her voice to a whisper. "Juli asked me to see if I could get into his room and look around."

"Great idea," Dave agreed. "All it takes is a master key."

"What if he catches me?" The very thought of the scowling red-haired man finding her in his room took Shannon's breath.

"He won't," Dave said confidently, although his serious expression didn't change. "He's downstairs right now helping clean up. Hey, do you want me to investigate Payne's room?"

Shannon slowly shook her head. "N— no. I have more reason to be in the rooms here than you do." Her voice wobbled.

"We just need to make sure we don't get caught." Dave's eyes gleamed. "How about this? When you go upstairs, make sure you open another room besides Payne's. I'll stand guard at the top of the stairs on this floor. Anyone who goes to the third floor will have to get by me." He grinned and flexed his muscles. "If Payne shows up, I'll ask him to help me move a dresser or something. It will give you time to hide in the unoccupied room."

"Think it will work?"

Dave looked solemn. "It has to. Juli can't go on being scared all the time." The way he said her friend's name made Shannon feel Juli didn't have to worry about Amy stealing Dave's affections.

Five minutes later, she unlocked both Andrew Payne's door and the room across the hall. Her heart thumped, bumped, and roared in her ears like a series of explosions. Grand and Dad would be furious if they knew what she was doing. "It's for a good cause," she told her conscience.

She stepped inside Payne's room. Her feet glued themselves to the soft carpet. Electronic equipment even her inexperienced eyes recognized must be state-of-the-art covered the desk, dresser, and table by the window. The telephone didn't look like other phones. A multitude of wires led to and from it. A computer sat nearby.

"Mr. Payne, could you help me move the dresser in my room?" Dave's loud call floated up to the reluctant spy. "I dropped something behind it and Ted's busy helping downstairs."

Shannon fled into the hall, hurriedly

locked the door, and crept into the unoccupied room, automatically locking it behind her. She leaned against it. Who was Andrew Payne, anyway? What would he do to her if he found out she'd been in his room? Did she dare ask Grand to make him leave? How could she, without admitting she'd sneaked into their guest's room?

Footsteps sounded on the staircase and in the hall. A key rattled in the door of Andrew Payne's room. Shannon strained to hear but couldn't tell whether he had gone inside or not. An eternity later, her hand dropped to the doorknob. Surely it must be safe to go.

The knob moved beneath her hand.

Terror filled her. *Please, God . . .*

The doorknob went back to normal position. The sound of retreating steps told Shannon she was alone on the third floor. Or was it a trick? She dared not move. A long time later a voice so low she barely heard it spoke in the hall. "Shannon?"

Drenched with perspiration, she finally managed to unlock the door, step outside, and lean against the wall.

"Are you all right?" Dave asked. "Payne's gone outside."

Shannon still didn't trust Payne. On tiptoe, she led Dave down the stairs. Would she ever again be willing to go to the third floor?

In the privacy of the den, she dropped to a chair. "I'm for bein' more scared than ever."

"What did you find?" Dave knelt beside her.

Running steps in the hall brought them to their feet. The next instant, Juli burst in, pushing the door closed behind her. "I am so glad you're here! You'll never believe —" A thunderous knock on the door cut her short.

Juli grabbed Shannon's arm and hissed, "It's Mary. She has a gun!"

Dave sprang between them and the door. "Who is it and what do you want?"

"Andrew Payne. Let me in. Now."

"Open the door, Dave," Juli cried in a ragged voice. "I've had it with him and that sister of his who isn't."

Dave took one look at her and obeyed.

Payne stalked in, closed the door, and leaned against it. He folded his arms over his chest. "This has gone far enough." A scowl worse than any he'd previously worn spread over his set face. "Which one of you girls was in my room?" He glared at Juli, then fixed his gaze on Shannon. "It was you, wasn't it? Your friend hasn't been back long enough."

Shannon stood paralyzed. How could he

know? He hadn't seen her.

Did Andrew Payne read her thoughts? He smiled unpleasantly. "Little girls who pry shouldn't wear perfume," he advised. "I knew someone had been there the minute I stepped inside. It wasn't my sister."

"How come your sister carries a gun?" Dave took a step forward, hands clenched into fists. "How come you've got enough equipment upstairs to stock an electronics store?" He refused to be stared down.

Payne slowly reached inside his shirt and held out a leather case.

"FBI?" Juli gripped Shannon's arm until it hurt. Pieces of the puzzle fell into place, then shattered into new formations, like kaleidoscope changes.

"If you tell anyone about this, you will destroy months of planning," Payne warned. "Trust me. There are lives at stake, more than you can know. We may never get another chance to stop what's happening." Truth rang in every word.

"At least tell us about the gray man," Juli pleaded.

"Don't worry about him." He uttered a fake-sounding laugh.

Anger roused Juli from the daze she'd gone into at learning who the inn "guest" really was. "What about Mary and her gun?"

"She's the best woman detective I know. She's carrying that gun for your protection," Andrew quietly told her.

"Then I really am in danger." It came out flat, but Juli felt fear tighten in her stomach. Dave and Shannon's faces showed they felt the same.

"I have to be honest. You could be, although we're doing all we can to prevent it." Compassion lightened his solemn face. "Be very careful. Don't wander around unless the boys are with you. Use your dramatic talent, all of you, and don't tell anyone what you've learned today. I have your word?"

Juli wordlessly held out one hand. Strength flowed into her from Andrew Payne's warm clasp. He shook hands with the others, and commented, "Keep your eyes open, your mouths shut, and report even the slightest suspicion to me. If you discuss this among yourselves, make sure you aren't overheard. Walls really do have ears." He opened the door and slipped out, leaving Dave and the girls staring at the empty hall outside the open doorway.

Until now, Juli had believed she was the world's best secret-keeper, with Shannon running a close second. Still, she came close to blurting out Andrew and Mary's identities a half-dozen times. Shannon said she had the same problem. "I have it on the end of my tongue all the time," she confessed.

"Tip of your tongue," Juli reminded.

"The tip is the end," Shannon answered. "Maybe it will be better when we go back to school."

"I doubt it," Juli said with such pessimism that Shannon's eyes opened wide in astonishment. Juli rolled over on her bed and didn't explain. Ever since she found the telltale piece of paper in the snow outside the kitchen door in Bellingham, she'd played ostrich in the sand. She refused to believe it could mean what the words hinted. No matter how many cops were what Dad always referred to as dirty, he wasn't — or hadn't been — one of them. She knew that beyond the shadow of a doubt.

Oh, yeah? a skeptical little voice prodded. *Then how come you don't show the message to your mom? Or Dave and Shannon? Or Andrew Payne?*

"Shut up!" Juli told the voice. "Just shut up and leave me alone." It didn't. She had no need to reread the words *This is the last time!!!* with their extra exclamation marks. They played a background accompaniment to whatever she happened to be doing. Again and again she wondered, *When was the message written?* The condition of the

160

paper indicated it had been some time ago, but lying in snow even for a short time would age the paper.

One good thing came out of Juli's turmoil. Step by faltering step, she slowly started back to where she'd left God. Ever since she admitted her complete helplessness and asked for His help on that unforgettable trip back from Bellingham, Juli had felt closer to Him.

On New Year's Eve, the house party's last full day at Skagit House, everything fell apart. Mom discovered Juli clutching the note. Juli knew there was no use trying to pretend, but she ached inside when her mother read it. "I — I don't know why anyone would have it now," Juli babbled. "The penciled words aren't even smudged, although the others are, and —"

"What are you saying?" Shock spread over Mom's face.

"I don't think Dad ever died."

"He would never be cruel enough to vanish and let us think he'd died." Mom's tears fell onto her shaking hands.

"What if he couldn't help himself?" She regretted saying it the minute it came out. "Don't look like that, Mom. It's probably nothing."

"Your father was the most honorable man

alive," Mom cried. "If you think he could ever be involved in something shady, then you never knew him at all!" She marched out of the room, leaving Juli miserable. Would the creeping horror that never seemed to stop claim her and Mom — and endanger everyone they knew?

Chapter 13

"The best of times. The worst of times." The words ran through Juli's brain like the lyrics of a popular song. Dave and Shannon's strong support helped. Mom's hurt look every time she glanced at Juli didn't. Neither did an incident on New Year's Day. Sean Riley drove Mom and the luggage home late that afternoon. Dave crowded Juli, Ted, and Shannon into his Mustang. Before they reached Bellingham, darkness fell, bringing with it the inevitable after-holiday letdown. Juli had never felt more depressed.

"Thanks," she called from the porch when the boys and Shannon left.

"See you." The Mustang pulled away from the curb.

Juli stumbled inside, glad Mom had arrived first. After what happened when she came in with Mary that time, the last thing she wanted was to be alone.

"Give me the paper you found and we'll lock it in the desk in the study," Mom said, once they'd unpacked. "It's a good thing we have one more day's vacation from school. Tomorrow we're going to the police." She set her lips in a straight line. "I refuse to let whoever is harassing us continue."

"Okay." Juli didn't dare suggest calling Andrew and Mary. Doing so would be breaking faith. She followed Mom to the den, watched her remove the top drawer and tuck the paper into the tiny space behind it before locking the desk. A little smile crossed Juli's face. How excited she had been all those years ago when Dad first showed Mom and her the secret hiding place! "See?" He had fitted a note from Juli into it and closed the drawer. "No one except the three of us will ever know it's there." When Juli determined to one day write mysteries, she decided some of the clues would be found in such a hiding place.

After a quick shower, Juli headed for bed. She tossed and turned. What would giving the message to the police mean? She hugged her friend Clue and brokenly whispered, "God, was Dad dirty? I don't want to believe he was a crooked cop, but I have to face facts. It would explain some things. Like the way his partner Baker acted when he came to tell us Dad wouldn't be coming home. Does he think Dad was involved in something? Do the rest of the force? Is that why they won't tell Mom and me anything?" Fierce pride rose within her. "Well, if they do, they can just unthink it. Please, God. Help me prove him innocent."

Juli fell asleep before resolving her conflict. Tomorrow would be a hard day and she was just too tired to consider it.

A quiet, observant officer who said his name was Wilson arrived shortly after breakfast in response to Mom's request for someone to come to the house. "Mrs. Scott, I understand you feel something unusual is going on. Tell me, please."

Mom, with Juli's help, repeated everything she knew. She ended, "Juli found a mysterious message lying in the snow," and led the way to the den. She unlocked the desk, pulled out the top drawer and stared. "That's strange. It doesn't seem to be here." She ran her fingers across the small space.

"It has to be!" Juli protested, although a sickening feeling hit her like a truck. "I watched you put it away and lock the desk. Maybe it fell behind the other drawers." She lifted them out and found nothing. The note had disappeared.

Detective Wilson bent over the lock. "I see no signs of it being forced. How many keys are there and who has them?"

"There are only three." Mom turned pale. "Mine, Juli's, and the one my husband carried."

Juli's arms prickled as if bugs crawled up and down them. It got worse when the detective asked, "Where are your husband's personal effects?" Mom stared and didn't answer, so he added, "You did get them, after the funeral?"

"No. Not even his wallet. They said they weren't available."

"*Who* said?" Wilson's voice cracked like a whip.

"Headquarters. Gary's supervisors," Mom replied.

Detective Wilson's face closed with the speed of light. "Someone used a key to this desk. I'll have the house checked for signs of breaking and entering."

The officers he summoned found nothing. *Why am I not surprised?* Juli wondered. Long after she repeated both sides of the note to Wilson and the police, Juli stood staring at the desk. Someone obviously had a key to it and the Scott house. More frightening, how could that person steal a note from a place only three people knew existed? And how had the alarm system been defeated? Unless, of course . . . Juli broke off. Had someone, maybe the gray man, learned about the alarm and the hiding place?

"Not from me," she muttered. "Or Mom. That leaves Dad. But how?" At bedtime Juli wrote in her journal,

Someone wants a soiled message badly enough to break and enter, a crime punishable by law. The $100,000 question is: Who? I can't tell Mom my suspicions. She has enough to worry about, even though the locksmith installed all new locks and the electrician tested the alarm system. I wonder if deadbolts can stop a gray man, if he's the one who took the note.

School started again and caught Juli up in homework and basketball games. It also reduced the number of hours she spent brooding over the mystery surrounding the Scotts, Rileys, and Skagit House. The Hillcrest Pirates won some games and lost others. Once Juli thought she saw Andrew Payne high in the bleachers, but wrote off the idea. Why would he be at a ball game? Another time she suspected she saw Mary at the mall. Before she could call Shannon's attention to her, the woman vanished. Juli couldn't be sure it had been Mary.

Juli worked hard on her character sketch

of Ryan Riley. She earned an A and high praise from Mrs. Sorenson. "He's real, Juli," her teacher wrote on her paper. "Keep up the good work."

Shannon and her father insisted on Grand coming in for a special celebration at a well-known seafood restaurant on Chuckanut Drive. The Rileys and Scotts drove around curving hills to an elegant converted Victorian-style mansion over-looking the bay. To the girls' surprise, Dave Gilmore and Ted Hilton waited at the entrance. "I'm glad Mom had us dress up," Juli whispered. "They are so cool!"

Especially Dave, her heart added. His blond hair and blue eyes showed up well against his dark suit, white shirt, and patterned tie.

"So are we," Shannon bragged in a low voice. "That blue is perfect on you and white is one of my best colors." She squeezed Juli's arm. "This is some place."

"You're telling me!" Juli tried to act nonchalant, as if every time she went out to eat a waiter stood with a towel over his arm and reeled off the choice of entrées. She secretly felt their bill might rival the national debt.

"This cooking is almost as good as at Skagit House," Dave remarked after tasting his fresh salmon steak and parsley potatoes.

"Flattery will get you everywhere." Shannon's eyes twinkled. "Juli and I are going back during the long weekend coming up. Want to join us?"

"Yes!" Dave smiled at Juli, seated next to him. "The basketball team has a game on Friday night, but I can come up the next morning."

Ted coughed. "If anyone wants to take pity on a poor, lonely orphan, I just happen to be available." He tried to look pitiful and failed miserably. "Dad has a meeting in Seattle. Mom and Amy are going with him to hit the stores."

"For us you'd give up shopping?" Shannon innocently inquired.

He grinned. "Yeah. I also got an underwater grade on my last trig test."

"Underwater grade?" Dave looked at him suspiciously. "What's that?"

"You know. Below *C* level." Ted roared.

"You're pathetic," Dave told him. The girls groaned and the adults laughed.

Shannon fixed a stern gaze on Ted. "Promise to study at the Skagit House?"

Ted smirked. "I have this friend who gets straight A's in math class, even though she can't quote things right. I thought maybe she'd give me a few hours of help so I can go on being the star of the Hillcrest Pirates basketball team."

"Sneaky," Shannon accused. "I guess I can, for the good of the cause."

"What cause?" Juli put in. It felt great to be lighthearted and have fun, instead of looking over her shoulder all the time to see if a gray man followed her.

" 'Cause I asked her to," Ted smugly replied. They all laughed.

During the chocolate mousse — Ted told Shannon she'd probably call it *mouse* — someone stopped at their table. "Hello there," an amused voice said.

Juli dropped her dessert spoon and turned. Andrew Payne stood behind her. She blinked. Could the gorgeous woman with him be *Mary?* Her turquoise silk dress silently shouted "Nordstrom's finest." Mom had priced a similar dress and left it on its padded hanger on a recent shopping trip with Juli. Mary's upswept hair with a few dangling curls made her look younger, more feminine. No wonder when Andrew turned to her, his eyes lit up like twin spotlights.

The FBI man also looked different. Used to seeing him in warm winter clothing, Juli checked out his dress suit. Impressive. It took an expert tailor to get a fit like that.

"She sure changed." Ted broke the silence after the others left and were seated at a table out of hearing distance. "He doesn't act very brotherly, does he? I can't imagine looking at Amy the way he does Mary!"

Juli's napkin slid off her lap to the floor. Both she and Dave reached for it. He took advantage of the brief confusion to whisper, "Those two had better watch it if they don't want to blow their cover." He gave Juli the napkin and squeezed her hand. "Don't let them being here spoil your party."

Warmed by his touch, she gulped and straightened. "Okay, people, let's talk about vacation. Is John going to feel left out if he isn't invited?"

"Where have you been since Christmas?" Ted demanded. "Mars? John wised up and is paying attention to Molly. You know, the speckled one at church."

"Not speckled, freckled. She's great," Shannon told him.

"John deserves a girl like that." Ted looked apologetically at the older members of the party, who had been sitting back enjoying the others' chatter. "Don't get me wrong. I'm not putting Amy down. She just needs someone who won't give in to her." He grinned tormentingly at Shannon. "Sort of like you."

Shannon sniffed. "Just remember, she who laughs last, laughs hardest."

"*And* best!" Ted admitted after the laughter died. "No one can ever get ahead of you, as long as you keep coming up with Rileyisms." They kidded all the way home in the Mustang. Again, Juli rejoiced over being able to feel carefree for a few hours. Even Andrew and Mary-whoever-she-was couldn't erase the special evening with Dave and the others; definitely a *best-of-times*. When Juli curled up in bed, she took her journal and wrote:

I haven't seen the gray man for a long time. On the other hand, the fog has been so heavy, he could be standing outside my window this very minute and I'd never know it. Nice thought. It makes my skin crawl. I haven't noticed a UPS van, either. Maybe I'm just getting so used to them being around, I don't see them. I wonder: Will he be at the Skagit House? Andrew and Mary will. Grand said they already made reservations. I don't know if it makes me feel better or worse. I'll have protection, but the thought that I need bodyguards is pretty scary.

The day before the Rileys and their friends left for Skagit House, the weather turned unseasonably warm. "It's awfully early for a chinook," Juli told Shannon.

"That's Indian for 'warm wind,' right?"

"Yeah. We could be in for a real flood." Juli remembered her dream and shivered, but nothing compared with what she felt when she stood on the riverbank. The chinook had brought down snow from the mountains and turned every stream, creek, and trickle into small rivers. They roared into the Skagit, changing it to a raging torrent of mud and debris. By Saturday night its song had become a warning scream. Sandbars where Juli and Shannon had built campfires and shared dreams for the future were gone. Cottonwoods torn from the bank smashed into other floating logs. The same greedy, sucking river that haunted Juli in her dreams now writhed and devoured the lower land, then licked at the base of the bluff below Skagit House.

Juli finally turned from its rowdy beauty, feeling compelled to check the birch clump. No brown van, but later in the afternoon she saw the gray man, half-hidden in the trees behind Skagit House. Waiting. Watching. Always watching. Suddenly she'd had it. Andrew Payne laughed him off. Others didn't see him. Today things would be different. Should she ask Shannon or Dave to help? No. Even to gain a witness, she wouldn't involve them in possible danger.

She slipped out after dinner, glad for her raincoat, and the downpour guaranteed to keep the few other guests inside. Out the back door. Around the building, keeping clumps of trees between her and the inn. No gray man. She might as well take another look at the flooding Skagit. Avoiding puddles, she reached the special point on the bluff where she always stood to watch the river.

The mocking bellow increased. She turned away, suddenly wanting to get back inside the brightly lit inn. She'd been crazy to come out in the rain. A slight movement beneath her feet warned her. She sprang back. Had the river weakened the side of the bluff? Too scared to scream, Juli pictured herself hurtling to certain death. No one would ever know what happened to her.

She gathered her strength and ran. Back from the bluff. Back from the river. A chunk of earth behind her broke and slid. She couldn't outrun the danger!

"Juli. Here." Strong arms reached for her through the murk and tore her away from ground that gave way beneath her feet. Someone picked her up and carried her. Juli

174

closed her eyes and clung to the racing figure's rough shirt. When her rescuer reached firm ground far back from the treacherous edge of the crumbling bluff, he set her down. Juli opened her eyes in time to see a familiar gray figure hurrying into the trees, shoulders bent and face hidden.

"Wait!" She started after him, determined not to let him go.

"Juli, stop." Andrew Payne spun her around. *"You can't go after him."*

"I have to!" she shrieked. "He saved my life. He . . ." Tears held back for weeks as she tried to be brave for Mom rivaled the force of the flood.

Andrew pulled her close. He mopped her face with a huge handkerchief and led her toward the inn. "Sorry to put you through this, but it's the only way."

She stumbled and nearly fell. "Please, Andrew," she wailed. "Let me go."

"No! You realize neither Shannon nor Dave are to know about this?"

Steel would bend sooner than Andrew Payne. His voice gave Juli the creeps.

"If you rush inside and spill what happened just now, it won't make things easier. It will also endanger your family and friends. Trust me a little longer."

She shivered in the night air and bitterly

asked, "What else can I do?"

Andrew took her to the back door. He checked both ways. "Now, get out of your raincoat and into the toughest, most important role you'll ever play."

Somehow Juli made it upstairs undetected, too numb to do anything but obey.

Chapter 14

After an Academy Award-quality performance that brought looks of approval from Andrew and Mary, Juli's fears came again. Drenched with sweat, she sneaked to the shower and let warm water and desperate prayers wash away the terror. The next afternoon, when Shannon suggested driving up the river road to Darrington, Juli secretly rejoiced. Anything to get away from Skagit House.

"Sorry Mary and I can't go," Andrew said. "We're going to Bellingham."

Juli's brain switched to fast forward. How come they were leaving just when things were supposedly reaching a crisis point? Maybe they weren't really FBI. After they drove away, she said, "I don't think I'll go. I have an idea for a story."

"You have to write it now?" Shannon sounded totally disbelieving.

"Mrs. Sorenson says if you don't practice self-discipline and get it down while it's there, you'll lose it." *She did say that,* Juli told her objecting conscience.

"I'll stay, too," Dave said. "It won't take you all day. We can hike later."

Shannon sent an I-don't-understand, we'll-talk-later look at Juli then asked, "Dad? Mom? Grand? You're coming, aren't you?"

Mom smiled. "Wouldn't miss it. If we come back at dusk we may see deer."

The Skagit House felt strangely quiet after they left. The few guests who came on Friday had tired of the rain and checked out just after lunch. "Let's have it, Juli. You didn't really stay here to write a story, did you?" Dave asked.

She hadn't actually promised Andrew she'd keep quiet. Too many months without answers made Juli confess, "Something's going down. Soon. I wasn't supposed to tell, but Andrew and Mary bailed out. I can't handle it by myself!"

Dave gave her an encouraging hug. "You know you can tell me anything."

"Even that I think the gray man is my father?" she whispered.

Dave's arm dropped. Shock spread over his face. "Your father's dead, Juli!"

Her heart dropped to her toes. "I don't know why, or how, or where he's been," she cried. "I just know when the gray man snatched me back from the edge of the bluff before it crumbled into the river last night, he had to be Dad."

Dave's jaw dropped. "The river? You could have been killed!" He put his arms around her and rested his chin on top of her head. "Thank God he was there." He hesitated. "If you're that sure, I believe you."

"Th— thanks." She pulled free and reached for a tissue.

"So what do Scott and Gilmore, P.I.s, do next?" Excitement filled Dave's eyes.

"Search. Everywhere. That's why I stayed here."

Two hours later Dave complained, " 'Easier said than won,' to quote Shannon. From basement to attic, we've turned up zip."

Juli sighed and wiped her hot, dirty face. "Searching's dirty work, isn't it?"

"What about the other buildings: barn, garage, pump house?" Dave scrubbed at a streak of dirt. "We're so used to having city water, we forget about pump houses."

"That's why the water here is so good. It comes from an underground stream about eighty feet down." Juli glanced at the clock. "We have to hurry or the family will wonder why we look like pigs wallowing in the mud." She grabbed the household keys from a kitchen hook and stepped outside with Dave.

The barn and garage gave no clues. By the time the two investigators headed for the pump house, screened from the house by cottonwoods, shadows lay heavy upon the lawn. Juli felt uneasy. "Maybe this isn't such a good idea."

"We can't quit now," Dave said. "This is the last place to search." He fitted a key from the ring Juli handed him into the lock. The door of the pump house swung in noiselessly. "Interesting." Dave poked a finger against a hinge and stared at his fingers. "Someone's kept this well-oiled."

Juli wanted to yell at him to lock the door and leave. Instead, she gritted her teeth and told herself to stop acting dumb. She'd been in the eight-foot-square, windowless building many times. She'd gone down the steps under the center trapdoor with Grand to check the pipes that glistened in the glow of an electric trouble light he plugged in above. Now the place looked dismal and frightening.

Dave hit the light switch and glanced around. "Nothing on the top level." He raised the trapdoor and peered down. "Any electricity down there?"

Juli plugged in the trouble light and

handed it to him. When he said, "Want me to go first?" she climbed down into what felt like another world, accompanied by the steady hum of the pump motor that kept the water tank filled.

"No luck." Dave sounded disappointed. "Let's go."

She scrambled up the steps, glad to be out of the small, moist space, and sighed when Dave replaced the trapdoor cover. "I guess I'm not as daring as Nancy Drew. I don't really like poky, dark places."

"Couldn't be any blacker than my hands. We'd better hit the showers." They stepped outside. Dave locked the door. "Dark out here, too. We should have brought a flashlight." He reached for Juli's hand. "Once we get to the lawn, we'll have the yard lights. They come on at dusk, don't they?"

She nodded, stumbled, and knew they were off the path. The steady rhythm of the pump motor continued. Juli stopped and tightened her grip on Dave's hand. "Why does the motor keep running when we're the only ones here?"

"Maybe someone left a faucet dripping." Dave laughed. "The pump will run even harder after I get done with my shower."

Unconvinced, Juli felt her way toward the lawn. "Where's the yard light?"

"The bulb must have burned out." Dave nearly fell over her when she stopped and stared across the darkened area ahead of them.

"In all the outside lights?" she asked skeptically. "There isn't a glimmer from here to the inn. There are lights in the house, so the electricity can't be off."

"I don't like this," Dave said close to her ear. "It's just too coincidental with Andrew and Mary leaving for Bellingham. Shall we make a run for the house?"

Juli's teeth chattered with excitement. The never-ending pump sang on, beating into her brain. "Let's go back to the pump house. The motor would never run this long for just a leaking faucet." She tried to control her frightened breathing. "Don't turn on the lights," she warned when they reached the pump house and went in. "Shut the door, plug in the trouble light, and point it down."

They descended the steps for a second time and checked every inch of the small space. Just when Juli was ready to give up, she noticed an odd-shaped piece of metal jammed into the machinery. Thinner than a dime, the flat disc kept the motor from shutting off. She automatically reached to remove it.

"Wait." Dave grabbed her hand, blue eyes enormous. "Don't take it out. It must be a signal. No one must know we're here."

"So who's around to hear us?" Juli protested. Then she heard a new humming sound. It grew louder and more menacing each second. "What's that?"

"We have to get out of here!" Dave said hoarsely. "Hurry."

Juli ran up the steps with him right behind her. He switched off the trouble light and opened the door. Juli's mouth felt dry.

Dave pushed past her. "Hang in there. We'll make it." They did. Clear to the clump of cottonwoods. "Ring-side seat," he muttered.

Juli stifled a nervous giggle. Sweat soaked her forehead until the danger-laden night wind lifted her hair, cooling her hot face and helping to quiet her pounding heart.

Dave held Juli's arm with one hand, parted branches with the other. A light flickered near the main road. It grew brighter, steadier, until it stopped less than twenty feet from where they lay. "You got the money?"

Juli's blood froze at the harsh demand. A gruff voice, obviously disguised, said, "Not so fast." Her world crashed. Dad — alive and involved in what must be a drug deal?

Why had God let her find it out? Juli gave a small cry, like a wounded bird. The next instant Dave's hand covered her mouth.

"What was that?" the first voice hissed. Somewhere, at some time, Juli had also heard *that* voice, but she couldn't hear well enough to identify it now.

"Night noises. There's no one here." The careless laugh chilled Juli.

"Hey, Shorty, bring the stuff." Scuffling sounds. A third fearsome shadow, making a blotch on the grass. A thud. A flare of light. A man knelt with his back to Dave and Juli and threw open a large case. "Enough drugs to give you a new life. Where's the cash?" He snapped the case shut.

"Here." The gray man handed over a briefcase and seized the drugs.

No, no, no! With superhuman strength born from pain and denial, Juli broke free from Dave's restraining arm. She burst into the circle of light and ran straight for the gray man, screaming, "Why? Why did you do it?"

His face twisted. "Go back!" he yelled.

The figure with his back to Juli turned. She staggered and nearly fell. No wonder she recognized his voice. The man with a crazed look in his eyes who stood as though paralyzed was Brian Baker, Dad's partner!

Shorty bellowed and clawed for a gun. The muzzle came up. A split second before it fired, Dave Gilmore knocked Juli to the ground and sprang past her, faster than he'd ever raced down the basketball court. He tackled Shorty, just as the cursing man fired. Gary Scott fell. Something gray flew through the air and landed on a bush. "Dad!" Juli screamed and scrambled to her feet.

It roused Brian from his state of shock. Face ghastly in the dim light, he cried, "Gary? No!" He launched himself at the struggling pair on the ground, tossed Dave aside, and grappled with the smaller man. Shorty tore free with strength born of desperation and fled — straight into Andrew Payne's arms!

Juli blinked in the sudden blinding light. Where had they all come from: Andrew, Mary, a half-dozen uniformed officers? Dave got up, rubbing a bruise on his face. Handcuffs snapped. Juli stumbled to Dad and dropped to the grass. Dark stains showed on his gray shirt. She felt nausea rise. "Are you —" Tears overflowed, cutting off her words. She clung to her father.

"Just my shoulder." His old smile looked strange on the gray face.

"No credit to you." Andrew Payne rudely

brushed her aside and opened Dad's shirt. "Thanks a lot for following orders and staying out of this!"

"You left," she accused, miserably aware his anger was justified.

"So you decided to play cop. Mary and I only pretended to leave. We watched you two so-called detectives, but couldn't blow our cover. Why'd you butt in?"

Juli felt scorched. Not Dave. "I didn't see you making any great moves, *Payne!*"

Dave's eyes blazed. Juli knew he was furious with Andrew for yelling at her.

"We don't interfere until the drug buy is complete," Payne snapped. "Now let's get Scott inside. Juli, prepare your mother when she gets home. Just say Gary's alive. Don't discuss the case until I get back tomorrow." He stalked off.

"Why didn't I know sooner that the gray man was Dad?" Juli brokenly asked Dave after Dad had been bedded down in a first-floor room with Mary as nurse.

"Easy. Here's a souvenir I plucked off a bush." He held out a gray wig.

Juli stared at it and cringed. "Throw it in the Skagit! I never want to see it again." Happiness over Dad's return changed to confusion. "I don't understand."

Dave rubbed his jaw. "Sounds to me like

your Dad's part of a successful sting operation. He will probably get an award. What a guy!" He looked awed.

Juli echoed it while she cleaned up and wondered how to tell Mom. All signs of trouble on the grounds had been erased before the laughing travelers returned. She followed Mom upstairs, perched on the bed, and silently prayed for help.

"You're awfully serious. Didn't the story idea fly?" Mom asked.

"I found one with a happier ending. Mom, do you still miss Dad? A lot?"

"More all the time. Sometimes I still turn, expecting him to walk in."

Juli blurted out, "What if he did?"

Mom turned chalky. "What are you trying to tell me?"

"Dad's alive. He was shot in the shoulder tonight, but he's fine."

Mom fell back, blue eyes enormous. *"Where is he?"*

"Downstairs." Juli followed her mother's racing figure. Anne jerked open the bedroom door and flew like a homing pigeon to the man propped up in bed. Juli ran to tell the others. "Shannon, Grand, everyone: Dad's alive!" Sean's fervent "Thank you, God" chased away any suspicion he'd had designs on Mom.

"Andrew will be back in the morning and tell us everything," Juli said.

Shannon hugged her, laughing and crying. "You were right. He wasn't dead."

Andrew and Mary — who turned out to be Mrs. Andrew Payne! — briefed them the next day, but Gary told most of the story from the couch next to Anne. He looked somber. "The best partner I ever had turned dirty. His wife had cancer — he needed money. I found out and Brian offered to cut me in. I consulted with Andrew and he told me to go along. Arresting Brian wouldn't get to the source.

"Someone grew suspicious. Instead of a drop, they planted an explosive device. God was with me that night. Just as I touched the door handle of the unmarked car, an inner alarm went off. I sprang backwards. The force of the blast threw me into the underbrush. I blacked out."

Andrew Payne picked up the story. "Baker never planned it," Andrew said, "yet he took advantage of the situation. With Gary out of the way, he could continue dealing. That's why we didn't let on we never found a body." He turned to Mom. "I know it sounds grotesque, but with Baker and the others believing Gary was dead, we knew they might get careless and give us a second crack at landing a whole lot bigger fish."

"It was a cruel thing to do!" Juli burst out.

"I know, but we had no choice." Compassion softened Andrew's face. "War, including the war on drugs, takes its toll on the innocent as well as the guilty."

"I'd lost all memory from the time of the explosion until months later. It's never come back." Dad grinned at Juli. "Mrs. Sorenson would tell you this is a plot weakness, but life is stranger than fiction. Anyway, I headed north. Something made me go to the FBI before I came home. They told me I was dead and buried!"

Mom gave a little cry of distress and he patted her hair. "At first I refused to stay dead, but as Andrew said, we are in a war. I prayed about it and decided a few more weeks wouldn't matter that much. It might also save lives." His voice grew husky. "If I'd known it would take this long, I'm not sure I'd have agreed to disguise myself, keep watch over you from —"

"A brown van. Only sometimes I saw you and the van at the same time," Juli put in. "You dropped that message, didn't you?"

"Yes. I found it in my pocket in California and kept it with me. Andrew drove the van part of the time. He said I was a fool, that

Brian would recognize me at the actual transaction, even though we arranged it through another party. I counted on it being dark enough on the grounds for the wig, gray makeup, and dropping my voice to get me by. Anne, Juli, will you forgive me? I weighed your pain and fear against the possible death of others, including kids and teens."

Mom leaned on his good shoulder and Sean Riley cleared his throat. "Sounds pretty close to Jesus teaching the greatest love is laying down your life for others."

Juli thought of the long, hard months. She thought of how easily even kids could get drugs. "I'm just glad you're okay."

"We offered Baker immunity if he'd testify against some drug lords we've been wanting to nail," Andrew said. "After the trial, he will be in the Witness Protection Program. We get the big fish. He deserves a second chance for tackling Shorty tonight, although Dave was handling things pretty well."

"We'll pray Brian doesn't blow it." Dad yawned. "I need to get back to bed."

"But who broke in at the Skagit House," Shannon demanded, "and why?"

Andrew quietly said, "Mary and I did. Distractionary tactics. Sorry we made a mess, but you'll remember, nothing was damaged."

He added, "The local police knew, of course."

Juli burned to ask questions, but the set of Andrew's lips warned *case closed*. She bent to kiss Dad, then giggled. "Now I have a fantastic story I can't use. It's too unbelievable to be accepted as fiction, even though it all happened."

"*Mysterious Monday* won't be a book, but it does have a great ending," Shannon reminded. "Even though only we will ever know all the story."

"Besides, teen mystery heroines solve the crime and we didn't," Juli added.

"Beginning detectives aren't supposed to solve major crimes," Andrew barked. "Maybe someday I'll throw some mysteries your way." He grinned.

Juli had the feeling they'd be too unimportant to make good plots!

By mutual consent, she and her friends walked outside to check on the river, making sure to keep away from the edge of the bluff. It no longer threatened to overflow its banks. Sunlight stole through the clouds and lay like a benediction.

Shannon flung her arms wide. "Look, there's a rainbow." She lifted her face to the pink-stained sky. "My mother used to say it made her feel like God was smiling." Tears glittered. She blinked hard and looked around the little circle. "I'm so glad we're all here and safe. The old camp song about friends is really true, isn't it? Some are silver and the others a pot of gold."

Ted grinned, but no one laughed. Dave gave Juli a quick hug that said he couldn't agree more. True friendship *was* a pot of gold.

Juli watched the Skagit reflect the colors of the rainbow, feeling she had it all. Dad home. Mom ecstatic. Loyal friends. If God felt as happy to have her close to Him where she belonged as she did, He must be smiling. *She* certainly was!